PRAISE FOR *CONJUGAL LOVE*

"In other hands, these would be the ingredients of farce, but Moravia, who died in 1990 and is considered one of the preeminent Italian writers of the twentieth century, delivers something at once more bitter and more tender: a parable of marriage . . . that captures the essential opacity of even one's most intimate partner." —*The New Yorker*

"*Conjugal Love* is deceptively complicated, a string of intense moments, revelations, and doubts. Can we ever know the people we love? What lies at the heart of and drives our creativity? How terrifying would it be to really understand yourself?"
— *The Los Angeles Times*

"To read Alberto Moravia's *Conjugal Love* is to be transported to the lush landscape of 1930's Tuscany. But the pleasure that comes from this amazing little book rests squarely with Silvio, the beguiling protagonist who leads readers to the story's central conceit: he and his wife have agreed that they will not have sex until the young dilettante completes writing his masterpiece."
—*The Washington Times*

"Freshly translated . . . Moravia, in this *Contempt*-like setup, achieves a sly, convincing portrait in the voice of Silvio, whose love for Leda emasculates him, yet fuels his work."
—*Publishers Weekly*

"Moravia . . . is a master storyteller and his political commentary never overpowers his narrative. The beauty of *Conjugal Love* is that, politics aside, it can be read simply as a compelling tale of love and betrayal." —*Star Tribune* (Minneapolis, MN)

"*Conjugal Love* isn't some paean to romantic love or marital bliss—but it's not cynical either . . . *Conjugal Love* is not a happy tale, but it is a satisfying one. And very well told."
—*Complete Review*

ALBERTO MORAVIA

CONJUGAL LOVE

— *a novel* —

TRANSLATED BY MARINA HARSS

Other Press • New York

Originally published in Italian in 1951 as *L'Amore Coniugale.*
Production Editor: Mira S. Park
Text design: Natalya Balnova
This book was set in Janson text by Alpha Graphics of Pittsfield, N.H.

Printed in the United States of America on acid-free paper. For information write to Other Press LLC, 267 Fifth Avenue, 6th Floor, New York, NY 10016. Or visit our Web site: www.otherpress.com.

Library of Congress Cataloging-in-Publication Data

Moravia, Alberto, 1907-
[Amore coniugale. English]
Conjugal love / by Alberto Moravia ; translated by Marina Harss.
p. cm.
ISBN-13: 978-1-59051-221-0
ISBN-10: 1-59051-221-9
1. Sexual abstinence—Fiction. I. Harss, Marina. II. Title.
PQ4829.O62A8413 2006
853'.912—dc22

2006005942

TRANSLATOR'S NOTE

Fascism was a crucial experience for Alberto Moravia, which left a lasting, though not always explicit, mark on his conception of society and human relationships. He wrote his first novel, *Gli Indifferenti* (*The Time of Indifference*) in 1929 (twenty years before *Conjugal Love*), at a time when Mussolini was consolidating his power. It dealt with two themes which would return again and again in his novels and stories: the moral apathy of the bourgeoisie, and the crucial role of sexuality in human relations. Fascism derived its power and strength from the acquiescence of the middle class, and to Moravia, the two were deeply intertwined, a theme he developed in *The Conformist* (1951).

Conjugal Love is a book about the love between a man and his wife. The protagonists, Silvio Baldeschi and his beautiful wife Leda, are idle members of the haute bourgeoisie, staying at an isolated house in Tuscany sheltered from the world around them. At one point Silvio mentions that it is the year 1937, and with this tiny, seemingly throwaway revelation, Moravia carefully places the domestic drama in a larger context. Silvio himself does not think about Fascism, or about anything at all beyond his great existential dilemma. And in part, this is why he is doomed to failure.

What is Silvio's dilemma? He wants to love, and he wants to write. Here we return to another central theme of Moravia's work. Sexuality is essential to man's view of himself, and is often in direct conflict with his ability to love. Women, and their mysterious, threatening sexuality, are complete enigmas. In her book, *Alberto Moravia*, Jane E. Cottrell wrote that "in Moravia's world men never seem to understand women. The female is always portrayed as more complicated than she at first appears, and she remains mysterious to her lover no matter how much he tries to probe her secrets and to possess her." To make matters worse, in *Conjugal Love* and many of the novels that followed it, the male protagonists are often aspiring or struggling artists, for whom this quest for possession renders the act of artistic creation even more difficult. Sexuality and creation become dueling impulses in an existential struggle that seems to have no satisfactory resolution. Silvio is a perfect example: he wants to write a novel, and also to possess his wife. These two drives become so completely entwined that they cancel each other out, and he becomes convinced that he must make a radical choice to find the success without which he feels he will die.

Moravia does not romanticize this struggle for artistic creation, and finds subtle ways to undermine it. He confines his readers to the limits of Silvio's lucid but almost absurdly narrow point of view, leaving them to struggle to comprehend his reality (while giving them clues from the beginning that

Silvio's vision of things is terribly lopsided). Silvio is limited by his egotism, his neuroses, and perhaps most of all, by his underlying alienation and sense of failure as a writer and as a man. But despite the shadow cast over his story by this sense of defeat, the tone of the book is anything but solemn. Moravia has constructed a rigorous—and comic—exposition of Silvio's high-minded, manic analysis of his obsessions, which I have tried to capture in my translation. I have attempted to allow the reader to participate in the narrator's excessively rationalistic analysis of his every feeling, action, and thought and his irritating lack of good sense. Even so, Moravia is able to render Silvio sympathetic in spite of, and perhaps because of, his limitations. Silvio is not a complete fool. In fact, he is a lucid and competent critic, and his analysis of his own literary work, which comes near the end of the book, is brilliantly damning. Perhaps because of this intellectual honesty, his sense of failure is pathetic, slightly comical, and very human.

The focus of Silvio's obsession eventually becomes what he perceives as his wife Leda's dual nature, the contrasts ingrained in her character and her appearance: on the one hand, an instinctual sensuality, and on the other, a civilized, remote beauty, which she expresses in an attitude toward him that he describes as *buona volontà*. This phrase appears over and over in the novel, always with slightly different connotations. It could be translated as "concern," "goodwill," "generosity," "empathy," "benevolence," "consideration," and doubtless in countless other ways. Finding a suitable translation for it became my own obsession. I found that every word or formulation I considered carried its own associations, creating discordances here or there in the book. "Concerned" seemed too negative, "goodwill" too pious, "generosity" too specific, "empathy" too general. . . . *Buona volontà* is an extremely common, banal phrase in Italian, and so I felt that the word that replaced it in English must not call attention to itself or feel too obscure. After much reflection I settled on "kindness" and its close relative "kindliness." I decided to use two closely related words rather than one in order to capture the full range of meaning of *buona volontà* without stretching a single word beyond its habitual usage. It was also important that the word have positive connotations, and yet be flexible enough to be used ironically when needed, as in the sentence: "Her attitude [toward me] expressed what is usually called, not without a touch of disdain, kindliness." And finally, the word had to contrast well, and put in sharp relief, the other, more mysterious side of Leda's character as Silvio sees it: archaic, uncivilized, and decidedly unkind.

This unknown, unknowable aspect of the beloved is at the heart of the novel, and exposes the complex nature of conjugal love itself: is it an expression of instinct and passion, of self-interest and bourgeois complacency, or of a more pure, generous feeling, something perhaps akin to kindness?

—Marina Harss
December 29, 2005

CONJUGAL LOVE

CHAPTER I

TO BEGIN WITH I'D LIKE to talk about my wife. To love means, in addition to many other things, to delight in gazing upon and observing the beloved. And this means delighting not only in the contemplation of the beloved's charms, but also in her imperfections, few or many as they may be. From the very first days of our married life, I took an immeasurable pleasure in observing Leda (for that is her name), and I loved studying her face and her person down to the smallest gesture and the most fleeting expression. When we were married, my wife (later, after bearing three children, certain traits became, not exactly different, but somewhat modified) was just over thirty years old. She was tall, though not excessively so, with a face and body that were beautiful, though far from perfect. Her long, thin face had an ephemeral, lost, almost washed-out quality, like the classical deities in certain mediocre paintings, executed tentatively and rendered even more tentative by the patina of time. This singular quality, an ungraspable beauty which, like a speck of sunlight on the wall, or the shadow of a moving cloud on the sea, can disappear at any moment, surely had something to do with her hair, which was of a metallic blond color and hung messily in long tresses, suggesting the fluttering of fear or flight; and with her enormous eyes, which were blue and slightly slanted, with moist, dilated pupils, whose humiliated, evasive gaze, like her hair, suggested a guarded, frightened disposition. She had a large, straight, noble nose, and a wide red, sinuously drawn mouth, the bottom lip protruding over a smallish chin, hinting at a heavy, brooding sensuality. Hers was an irregular and yet very beautiful face, with a beauty, as I have said, that was ungraspable and that in certain moments and in certain situations, as I will describe later on, seemed to dissolve and even disappear altogether. The same could be said of her body. From the waist up she was as thin and delicate as a young girl; but her hips, belly, and legs were solid, strong, and well developed, imbued with muscular and carnal vigor. But the disharmony of her body, like that of her face, was neutralized by her beauty which, like a familiar intangible melody or a mysteriously transformative light, wrapped her from head to toe in a halo of perfection. Oddly enough, sometimes, as I gazed at her, I thought of her as a person with classical contours and forms, without defects, the essence of harmony, serenity, and symmetry. Such was the extent to which her beauty, which, for lack of another word I will call spiritual, deceived and seduced me. But there were moments when this golden veil was torn away, and in those moments not only did I see her numerous imperfections, but I observed a painful transformation of her entire person.

I discovered this in the first days of our marriage and for a moment I felt almost deceived, like a man who has married for money and discovers after the wedding that his wife is penniless. Often, a broad, mute grimace which seemed to express fear, anxiety, and withdrawal, and at the same time a mixture of repulsion and attraction, would distort her face. When this grimace appeared, the natural imperfections of her features stood out, so to speak, in a violent manner, giving her entire face the repulsive aspect of a grotesque mask in which certain features have been deliberately exaggerated to the point of caricature in order to create a particular, comically obscene or bizarre effect. This was especially true of her mouth, but also of the lines on either side of her mouth, and her nostrils and eyes. My wife applied bright red lipstick abundantly to her lips, and because she had a pale complexion, she also used rouge on her cheeks. When her face was in repose, these artificial colors were hardly noticeable; they merely complemented the color of eyes, her hair, and her complexion. But when the grimace appeared, the colors stood out, vivid and raw, and her whole face, which just a moment before had been serene, luminous, and classically beautiful, evoked the ridiculous, exaggerated features of a carnival mask, rendered almost obscene by the softness, heat, and vividness of live flesh.

Just like her face, her body had a way of belying the enchantment of beauty that enveloped it, by contorting itself repulsively. Her entire body would cringe, like a person who is afraid or revolted by something; like a mime or a dancer, she thrust her arms and legs forward in a gesture of defense and repugnance, but at the same time, her body arched in a gesture of invitation and provocation. She appeared to fend off an imaginary danger with her arms, and at the same time, with a vehement distortion of the hips, to suggest that this danger or assault was not completely repellent to her. The coarseness of the attitude, which was often accompanied by the grimace I mentioned earlier, made one almost doubt that one was seeing the same person who just a moment before had appeared so composed, so serene, so ineffably beautiful.

I said earlier that to love someone means to embrace everything about her, not only her beauty but, if it is present, her ugliness. The grimace and distortion of the body, while repulsive, soon became as dear to me as her usual beauty, harmony, and serenity. But love, at times, can create a lack of understanding; because even if it is true that there is a kind of love that involves comprehension, it is also true that there is another, more passionate kind that renders us blind when it comes to our beloved. I was not blind, but I lacked the clear-mindedness that can be attained in a long-term, timeworn, love. I realized that at times my wife could become ugly and coarse; I found this to be curious, and like everything about her, charming, and I did not see or care to delve beyond this observation.

I must say at this point that the grimace and convulsion occurred only rarely and never during our intimate relations. I do not remember a single occasion when a word or gesture of mine provoked the strange transformation of her face into a mask and of her body into that of a marionette. In fact, during our lovemaking she seemed to reach the apex of her astonishing, ineffable beauty. In these moments, the dilated and moist pupils of her large eyes conveyed a wounded, docile, sweet entreaty which was more expressive than any words; her mouth seemed to communicate, in the sensuality and sinuousness of her lips, an intelligent and capricious goodness; and her entire face responded to my gaze like a reassuring and mysterious mirror, graciously framed by her long blond tresses. Her body seemed to compose itself in its most graceful attitude, innocent and languid, defenseless and without shame, like a promised land offering itself, golden and unprotected, to the gaze of the passerby, its fields, rivers, hills, and valleys stretching out before him to the horizon. In contrast, the grimace and convulsion occurred in the most unexpected and insignificant moments. I remember a few instances: My wife has always been a great reader of detective novels. Well, when the plot was at its most engrossing and terrifying point, I would notice her face gradually contorting itself into a grimace, which disappeared only when she had reached the end of the passage. My wife also enjoyed gambling. We went together to Campione, Montecarlo, and San Remo; each time, after the bets had been made, as the roulette wheel turned and the little ball skipped over the numbers, my wife's face would rearrange itself in this indecent grimace. And even when she was simply threading a needle, or when she saw a child running alongside a ditch, in danger of falling in, or when a drop of cold water ran down her back—all of these events were enough to provoke the grimace.

But I would like to recount in detail two occasions in which it seemed to me that this singular transformation had more complex origins. One day we were in the garden of our villa in the countryside, and I was trying to yank out a tall, blooming weed, practically a shrub, which had somehow popped up in the middle of the gravel drive. It was not an easy task; the moist green plant seemed to have deep roots, and kept slipping through my fingers. I was intent on this task, but for some reason I raised my eyes toward my wife and was shocked to see her face and body transformed by the familiar coarse expression and contortion. At that moment, finally ceding to the weight of my body, the weed lurched out of the ground, revealing one solitary, long and robust root, and I fell backwards onto the gravel.

On another occasion we had invited some friends over for dinner to our home in Rome. Before the guests arrived, my wife, dressed in an evening gown, hair combed up, and wearing her jewels, decided to pay a visit to the kitchen to make sure everything was in order. I followed her. We found the cook cowering before the lobster, a huge beast armed with formidable claws and still half alive; she did not have the courage to take hold of it and plunge it into the awaiting pot. My wife approached the table without fanfare, grabbed the lobster by the back, and tossed it into the boiling water. In order to do this, she had to hold herself far from both the burner and the animal. But this need for prudence did not fully explain the appearance of the ugly, grotesque grimace on her face, nor the visible movement of her body which for a moment seemed to suggest a provocative swaying of the hips beneath the shimmering silk of her evening gown.

I must assume that my wife has contorted her face and body in this manner an infinite number of times in her life, and in the most disparate situations. Even so, a few facts remain indisputable. She never contorted her face or body when we made love. And these contractions were always accompanied by the most profound silence, a suspenseful silence more reminiscent of a repressed scream than of the stillness of tranquility. Finally, the grimace and contraction seemed to always result from the fear of an unexpected, sudden, rapid event. A fear which, as I have noted, was mixed with attraction.

CHAPTER II

UP TO THIS POINT, I have spoken only of my wife. Perhaps it is time for me to say something about myself. I am tall and thin, with an energetic face and prominent, narrow features. Perhaps, if one looked more closely, one might discover a weakness in the shape of my chin and the outline of my mouth. But even so, I have a strong, sincere face that is completely in contrast with my true personality, though it may partially explain some of my contradictions. Perhaps my fundamental characteristic is a lack of depth. Whatever I do or say at any particular moment, this action or pronouncement defines me completely, leaving me nothing in reserve if I am forced to back down. In sum, I am all front line, without an army or rearguard behind me. This explains my facile enthusiasms; any small trifle fills me with exaltation. But this enthusiasm is a bit like a horse that jumps over a hurdle without noticing that its rider has remained ten meters behind, in the mud. What I mean is that this enthusiasm is almost never supported by the effective internal force without which any enthusiasm dissolves into vague desires and rhetoric. It is also true that I am inclined to rhetoric, preferring words to action. My rhetoric generally has to do with the realm of emotion; I want to love and I often delude myself into believing that I am in fact in love, when I have simply uttered words of love, fervent, but still only words. In these moments I cry easily, I stutter and indulge in all the outward signs of an overwhelming emotion. But underneath these displays of fervor, there is often an acrid and even mean shrewdness or duplicity which is not a sign of strength, but rather the expression of my egotism.

For those who knew me only superficially, I was, before meeting Leda, what is now (and not, perhaps, for much longer) known as a "dandy." In other words, a man who is well-to-do enough not to have to work, and who is thus able to dedicate his time to the study and enjoyment of beauty in all its forms. This label was generally accurate, at least according to the role I played in public. But when I was alone, I was actually anything but a dandy; I was tormented by anxiety, always on the brink of despair. In the writings of Poe there is a tale that accurately describes my state of mind at the time. It recounts the adventure of a fisherman whose boat is pulled into the vortex of a whirlpool. His boat sails in circles around the edge of the abyss; above, below, and around him floats an endless stream of fragments from previous shipwrecks. He knows that as he turns he constantly approaches the bottom of the vortex, where death awaits him, and he is perfectly aware of the force which has produced the fragments that are spinning around him. Well, my life at that time could be described as a continual vortex. I was caught in the spirals of a black funnel, and above, below, and around me I could see all the things

I loved spinning with me. I could see the things that, in the minds of others, I lived for and that instead were being pulled down with me in that strange shipwreck. I felt myself spiraling round and round with all the beautiful, true things that have been created, and at every moment, without respite, I saw the dark center of the funnel, which promised a certain and inevitable end for me and for everything else. There were moments when the vortex seemed to become less vast, more shallow, and to turn more slowly, pushing me toward the calm surface of daily life. But at other times, the spiral became tighter, faster, and deeper, and then I descended further and further, along with all the creations of human art and reason; at these moments I almost hoped to be swallowed up forever. When I was young, these moments of crisis were frequent and I can say that between the ages of twenty and thirty, not a day went by that I did not ponder the idea of suicide. Naturally, I did not really want to kill myself (otherwise I would have done so), but this obsession with suicide was still the dominant color of my internal landscape.

I often tried to come up with a cure for my situation, and I soon realized that only two things could save me: the love of a woman and the act of artistic creation. It may seem a bit ridiculous to mention two things of this scale in such a casual manner, as if I were speaking of two common medicines to be acquired in a pharmacy. But my summary account reveals the great clarity of thought that I had achieved regarding the problems of my life. I felt that I had a right to love, like all men in this world, and I was also convinced that my tastes and the talent that in my most optimistic moments I believed myself to possess inclined me toward artistic creation.

But the fact was that I could never get past the first two or three pages of any composition, just as in my relationships with women I could never achieve a depth of feeling that convinced them or me. What hindered my sentimental and creative efforts was precisely my facile enthusiasm: it was quickly awoken and vanished just as quickly. How often a kiss stolen from reluctant lips, or two or three fervently scribbled pages led me to believe that I had found what I was seeking. But almost immediately I would slip into a verbose sentimentality that eventually drove my lady friend away, or as I wrote I would lose myself in sophism or surrender to an abundance of words, a momentary facility that belied the absence of real inspiration. I would start promisingly, deceiving myself and others, only to give way to a cold, generic flabbiness of style. Then I would realize that I had in fact never loved or written so much as desired to love and to write. Sometimes I met a woman who out of self-interest or compassion was willing to let herself be deceived and to deceive me in turn; once or twice a page seemed to bear my scrutiny and invited me to continue. But I do have one positive quality: a diffident nature that saves me from the path of self-deception. And so I would tear out the page or, with some pretext, break off relations with the woman. And so, amid such attempts, my youth drew to a close.

CHAPTER III

IT IS IRRELEVANT WHERE OR how I met my wife; perhaps it occurred in someone's sitting room, or perhaps it was at a holiday resort or another similar spot. She was close to my age and it seemed to me that in many ways my own life paralleled hers. In reality these parallels were few and superficial, and stemmed from the fact that, like me, she was well off and had the freedom to do as she pleased and lived among the same people I did, and in a similar manner. But to me, with my usual ephemeral enthusiasm, these similarities appeared significant, as if I had found a soul mate. When she was very young, she had been married in Milan, the city where she was born, to a man she did not love. The marriage had lasted a few years and then the two had separated and later divorced in Switzerland. From then on my wife had always lived alone. The thing that had immediately made me hope that I had finally found the woman I was looking for was her confession to me on the day I met her: she told me that she was tired of the life she had been leading and that she wanted to settle down in a relationship close to her heart. I thought I glimpsed in this confession—which she made with utter simplicity and without any hint of emotion, as if she were discussing a practical plan and not the wretched aspiration of one who had lived for years without love—a state of mind similar to the one I had experienced for so long. And at that moment, with my characteristic enthusiasm, I decided that she would be my wife.

I don't think that Leda is particularly intelligent, but despite this, and because of her measured manner, her air of experience, and her judicious blending of indulgence and irony, she acquired a mysterious authority in my eyes. Even the slightest gesture of comprehension or encouragement from her seemed precious and flattering. I convinced myself that I would be able to persuade her to marry me, but today I can say that she was the one who willed it, and that without her determination, the marriage would never have happened. We were still in the early days of our courtship, which I imagined to be long and intricate, when she—practically forcing the issue—gave herself to me. Had this gift come from another woman I probably would have perceived it as a sign of lightness and it would have elicited my contempt, but from her it seemed precious and flattering, as had her early indications of approval and encouragement. After I had possessed her, I realized that her mysterious air of authority remained intact and had even been increased by the awakening of my senses. Just as earlier she had gratified my need to be understood, now, with even greater and more instinctive intelligence, she gratified my desire. And thus I discovered that the ephemeral, unstable quality of her beauty corresponded to a similar quality in her soul. I never felt that I possessed her completely;

just when it seemed that I was beginning to feel sated, a gesture or a word from her would suddenly make me fear that I had lost her. These alternating states of possession and desperation continued, one could say, until the day we were married. By then I loved her ardently and I understood that I had to do everything in my power to keep this love from ending, as the previous loves had, in discouragement and emptiness. Driven by this fear, but reluctant and tormented by the feeling that my solution was perhaps too simple to be effective, I asked her to become my wife, certain that she would immediately accept. Instead, she responded with shocked refusal, as though my proposal had broken an obscure rule of etiquette. This refusal flung me to the deepest level of desperation. I left her, believing in my confusion that there was nothing more for me to do and that if I had any courage, this was the moment to kill myself. After a few days she called me, surprised, to ask why I had disappeared. I went to see her, and she greeted me with a soft and impudent reproach for giving up without allowing her the time to reflect. In conclusion, she said that she would accept to become my wife after all. Two weeks later, we were married.

For me that was the beginning of a period of complete happiness, the likes of which I had never known. I loved Leda passionately, and at the same time I feared that my love—or hers—would come to an end. And so I tried to bind our two lives together in every way, to create bonds between us. As I knew she had little education, I proposed a kind of course in esthetics, persuading her that she would enjoy learning as much as I would enjoy teaching her. I discovered that she was an exceedingly docile and attentive pupil, far more so than I had imagined her. Together, we established a plan of study and a schedule, and I took it upon myself to impart to her and aid her in the appreciation of all that I knew and loved. I don't know how closely she followed or how much she understood of what I told her; probably less than I believed at the time. But because of her singular and mysterious air of authority, I felt a sense of accomplishment whenever she said simply, "I like this music," or "This poem is beautiful," or "Read that passage again," or "Let's listen to that record one more time." At the same time, in our free moments, I taught her English. She made considerable progress in this subject because she had a good memory and a natural inclination for languages. Her inalterable good humor, sweetness, and willingness rendered our discussions, reading sessions, and lessons appealing and precious to me. In a way, even though she was the student and I the teacher, it was I who experienced all the trepidation of the pupil; and it was rightfully so, since the subject we were exploring was our love, and I felt as if each day I mastered it more and more completely.

Even so, the true foundation of our happiness, besides our now shared tastes, was our lovemaking. I have said already that her beauty, sometimes disturbed by an ugly grimace and contraction of the body, was never distorted during the act of love. I will add that my enjoyment of her beauty had become the pivot of the once dark and ominous, now luminously unhurried, regular vortex of my life. How many times, lying next to her in bed, I contemplated her naked body and was almost frightened to see how beautiful it was, and at the same time the degree to which it eluded definition, despite my insistent contemplation. How many times, as she lay next to me, her head resting on the pillow, I ran my fingers through and played with her long, smooth, blond tresses, attempting in vain to grasp the mysterious significance of the movement that caused them to flutter and tremble. How many times I gazed into her enormous blue eyes and asked myself what the secret of their soft, wounded expression might be. How often, after kissing her fervently, I studied the sensation of her lips on mine, hoping to penetrate the meaning of the slight, almost archaic smile which reappeared at the angles of her large, sinuous mouth, like the smile of a Greek statue. It seemed to me that I had discovered a mystery as deep as the mystery of religion, a mystery according to my own heart, through which my eyes and my mind, accustomed to the contemplation of beauty, could finally lose themselves and find peace in a pleasurable, infinite space. She seemed to understand how important this adoration was to me, and she let herself be loved with the same tireless docility, the same intelligent complacency with which she allowed herself to be instructed.

Perhaps, in the midst of this happiness, I should have been put on my guard by one particular aspect of my wife's attitude which I believe I have already alluded to: her kindness. Clearly, love was not as spontaneous in her as it was in me. And there was in her attitude toward me a clear, if mysterious desire to please, to gratify, and perhaps even to flatter. In other words, her attitude expressed what is usually called, not without a touch of disdain, kindliness. But such kindliness generally conceals something else which, if uncovered, reveals its falseness and hinders its effect, whether it is an assortment of innocuous worries or, in the worst case, a double nature or even treachery. But I accepted this kindliness as further proof of her love for me and did not at first attempt to discover what it concealed, or what it might signify. In sum, I was too contented not to be self-interested. I knew that for the first time in my life I was in love, and with my typical, somewhat indiscreet enthusiasm, I ascribed the feelings that filled me to her as well.

CHAPTER IV

I HAD NEVER MENTIONED MY literary ambitions to my wife, in part because I didn't believe she would understand them, but also because I was embarrassed to confess that they were only ambitions, or rather attempts which had never seen success. That year, we spent the summer at the shore, and toward the latter half of September we began to discuss our plans for the fall and winter. For some reason—perhaps in the context of a discussion about my long period of idleness following our marriage—I mentioned my sterile labors. "But Silvio, you've never mentioned this before," she exclaimed. I told her that I had never said anything because, at least up to that moment, I had never written anything that I felt the need to talk about. But, in her usual, kindly affectionate way, she induced me to show her something I had written. I immediately realized that her curiosity flattered me enormously, and that ultimately her opinion was just as or even more important to me than that of a professional man of letters. I was well aware that she was uneducated, that her tastes were uncertain, and that her approval or disapproval could have no real literary value; and yet I felt at that moment that my future as a writer depended entirely on her opinion. I resisted, pro forma, and then, after warning her several times that these were trifles which I myself had repudiated, I agreed to read her a brief story I had written a few years earlier. As I read it, I felt that the story was not as flawed as it had seemed to me in the past; I read on, my voice stronger and more expressive, every so often stealing a glance at her as she listened attentively without revealing her impressions in any way. When I finished, I thrust the pages aside and exclaimed, "as you can see, I was right, it was not worth mentioning." And I awaited her judgment with a strange feeling of anxiety. For a moment she said nothing, as if gathering her thoughts, and then she declared with peremptory firmness that I was very mistaken to deny my talent. She said that she had enjoyed the story, even if it had many flaws, and she elaborated and explained why. Hers was not—and how could it be?—the judgment of an expert, but even so, I felt strangely encouraged. It seemed to me that all her reasons, which were those of a normal person with normal tastes, could be as valid as those of the most refined literati, and that perhaps, after all, I imposed a level of perfectionism on myself which was more destructive than good; and finally, that perhaps what I had lacked up to that point was not talent but the encouragement which she was now lavishing upon me. There is always something humiliating and false about praise for one's successes from family members, in other words people whose affection renders them indulgent and partial. A mother, a sister, or a wife are always disposed to recognize in us the genius that others obstinately refuse to see, but at the same time their praise is never enough; at times it inspires more bitterness than clear disapproval from others. I did not feel this way where my wife was concerned. It seemed to me that she truly liked the story, independently of the affection she felt for me. In addition, her praise was discreet and specific enough that it did not seem to be merely the result of pity. Finally I asked her, almost shyly: "So you think I should keep going, keep trying?. . . . Think carefully before you answer. If you say to keep trying, I will . . . but if you say to give up, I will give up and will never put pen to paper again . . ."

She laughed and said, "This is a heavy responsibility."

I insisted: "Speak to me as if I weren't myself but a stranger . . . say what you really think."

"But I already told you," she answered, "you must keep trying."

"Really?"

"Yes, really."

She was quiet for a moment and then added: "In fact, listen . . . let's do this . . . instead of going back to Rome, let's spend a month or two in your villa in Tuscany . . . there you can work, and I'm sure that you will write wonderful things."

"But you'll be bored."

"Why? You'll be there . . . and it will be a change . . . it has been so many years since I spent some quiet time doing nothing."

I must say that what persuaded me was not so much her reasoning and her encouragement as a kind of superstition I felt. I thought that for the first time in my life a benevolent star was shining down on me, and I told myself that I had to do everything I could to advance this unexpected good fortune. With my wife I had finally found the love that I had aspired to for so many years in vain; perhaps now I would be blessed with literary creativity. I felt that I was finally on the right path, and that the beneficial effects of our meeting had not yet been exhausted. I embraced my wife and jokingly said that from now on she would be my muse. She did not seem to understand me, and asked again what my decision was.

I told her that, just as she had suggested, we would leave for my country house in a few days. A week later, we left the Riviera for Tuscany.

CHAPTER V

THE VILLA ROSE UP FROM a depression at the foot of a small ridge, on the edge of a vast, flat cultivated plain. It was surrounded by a small garden crowded with lush trees. Thus there was no view from any of the windows, even on the top floor, and one felt as if one was not on the edge of a plane punctuated by farmhouses and divided into fields, but rather in the depths of a great forest, in a lonely refuge. Not far from the house, on the plain, there was a large rustic village. The closest city, on the other hand, lay one hour away by cart, at the top of one of the mountains that loomed up behind the house. It was a medieval city, surrounded by crenellated walls, with palazzos, churches, convents, and museums; but as often happens in Tuscany, the medieval quarter was much poorer than the ugly modern village which had been built up by traffic routes down below in the plain. The house had been built perhaps a century earlier, judging by the size of the trees. It was a simple, regular building, with three stories and three windows on each story. In front of the house there was a gravel-covered driveway shaded by two horse chestnuts; a twisting path meandered from the driveway to the gate of the garden and from there, it ran alongside an old wall, to the main road. As I have said, the garden was small but lush and filled with shady nooks. On one side its edge was clearly defined, but on the others one could pass from the shade of the underbrush to the cultivated fields without crossing hedges or other obstacles. A few farm buildings were attached to the property, and the sharecropper's farmhouse rose up by the edge of the garden on a hillock from which one could enjoy a view of the entire plain. From the main house one could hear the calls of the farmers as they drove their oxen forward in their furrows. And often the sharecropper's chickens meandered in the garden and pecked their way up to the gravel driveway.

Inside, the house was filled with old furniture representing every style of the last century, from Empire to Art Nouveau. Its last inhabitant, my maternal grandmother, had died there at the age of almost a hundred; throughout her life, with the patience and hoarding instinct of an ant, she had collected enough furniture to fill a second house of equal size. The drawers, closets, and chests overflowed with an eccentric mass of objects: china, linens, knickknacks, rags, old papers, utensils, lamps, photo albums, and countless other things. The bedrooms were vast and dark, with canopy beds, gigantic chests of drawers, and murky family portraits. In addition, there were an unknown number of sitting rooms and a library filled with shelves of old books, for the most part volumes of patristics, almanacs, and magazine collections. There was even a small bare room with a billiard table, but the felt was ripped, and there were only a few cues, and no billiard balls. We moved about with difficulty among the creaking objects in this crowded space, as if the furnishings were the true inhabitants of the house, and we simply intruders. But I managed to clear some space in a sitting room on the second floor, keeping only its original handsome Empire furniture, and made it my study. We each chose a bedroom, and my wife took as her sitting room the parlor on the ground floor which contained the only two comfortable chairs in the house.

From our first day in the villa, we led a very regular life, like that of an industrious convent. In the morning, the elderly housekeeper brought a tray to my wife's bedroom and we had breakfast together; she sat in the bed, and I on a chair next to her. Then I retired to my sitting room, sat down at the desk and worked, or at least tried to work, until noon. Meanwhile, my wife, after lingering a while longer in bed, would get up, slowly and meticulously prepare her toilette and, while dressing, make a list of the cook's daily instructions. Around midday, I stopped working and went down to the ground floor where my wife awaited me. We had lunch in a small dining room, in front of a French window that opened onto the garden. After lunch, we had our coffee in the garden, in the shade of the horse chestnuts. Then we went up to our rooms for a brief rest. Teatime brought us together once again in the ground floor sitting room. After tea, we went out for a walk. There weren't many different paths to take. The cultivated parts of Tuscany are more like a garden, without benches or paths, than like open countryside. Either we followed a meandering path through the fields between one farmhouse and the next, or we walked along the grassy bank of a canal that crossed the plain from one end to the other; sometimes we walked down the main road, though never as far as the village or the city. When we returned from our stroll, which never lasted more than an hour, we had our English lesson and then, if there was time left over, one of us would read to the other. We ate dinner, and afterwards we read some more or talked. Finally, not too late, we went up to our rooms, or, more precisely, I followed my wife to her room. That was when we made love, and in fact it was the moment that our entire day had been leading up to. My wife was always willing and docile, and I had the sense that she was rewarding herself and me for the many quiet hours we had spent. In the rural night that peered in through our wide-open windows, the profound silence only rarely interrupted by the twittering of a bird—in that high, dark room, our love was quickly kindled and burned lastingly, silently, limpid, and alive like the flame from one of the old oil lamps that once lit these shadowy chambers. I felt that I loved my wife more each day, and that each night's ardor built upon and took strength from that of the previous night; she seemed never to exhaust the reserves of her affectionate and sensual generosity. During those nights, for the first time in my life, I felt that I had penetrated the true nature of conjugal passion: that odd mixture of violent devotion and legitimate lust, of exclusive and limitless possession, and pleasure in the confidence of possession itself. For the first time I understood the at times immodest feeling of ownership that certain men ascribe to the conjugal relationship, uttering the phrase "my wife" with the same tone as "my house," "my dog," and "my car."

What was not going well, despite the very favorable conditions, was my work. I wanted to write a novella or a short novel, and was fascinated by the subject I had chosen, the story of a marriage. It was our story, the story of my wife and myself, and I felt that it was already composed in my mind, divided and organized into single episodes, to be laid out with the greatest ease. But as soon as I sat down in front of the sheet of paper and tried to write, the story became confused. Sometimes the paper would be covered in erasures, or I would get through a page or two only to discover that I had simply accumulated a series of generic sentences, lacking any concreteness. Sometimes, after I had written only a few lines I would stop and remain still, absorbed before the white page, as if in deep reflection, but in reality my mind blank and my spirit inert. I have a highly developed critical sense, and for several years I have written criticism in journals and newspapers; I realized very quickly that not only was my work not advancing, but it was progressing more slowly even than before. At other times in my life I had been able to focus my mind on one subject and develop it, admittedly without ever reaching the level of poetry, but always achieving a clean, decorous style. But now I realized that not only was my subject eluding me, but so was my usual command of style. A malignant force was driving me to accumulate repetitions, solecisms, unclear limping formulations, uncertain descriptions, emphatic locutions, platitudes, and clichés. But above all I felt that my prose lacked rhythm, that regular, harmonious breathing that sustains its flow, just as meter sustains and regulates the motion of poetry. I remembered that at one time I had mastered this rhythm; in my own modest and limited way, it is true, but still it was sufficient. Now even this was missing; I stumbled, stuttered, lost myself in a tumult of discordances and stridencies.

I might have given up my work—since the love I felt for my wife was enough to ensure my happiness—if she had not incited me to persist. Not one day went by when she did not inquire with affectionate and insistent solicitude how my work was advancing. Ashamed to confess to her that it was not advancing at all, I would answer vaguely that it was coming slowly but surely. She seemed to ascribe the greatest importance to this labor, as if it were somehow her responsibility to do so, and each day I felt a greater responsibility to complete it, not for my own sake but for hers. It would be a sign of my love for her, a demonstration of the profound change that her presence had wrought on my life. This is what I had meant when, embracing her, I had whispered that from then on she would be my muse. Without realizing it, her daily questions regarding my morning's work inspired me to succeed, as a point of honor, just as in medieval fables ladies ask their cavaliers to bring back the golden fleece and destroy the beast; in these stories, the cavalier never returns downcast and contrite, empty-handed, to admit that he was unable to find the fleece or that he did not have the courage to face the dragon. This point of honor was rendered even more pressing and peremptory by the particular nature of the request: it was not the request of a highly educated woman, well-versed in the challenges of intellectual labor, but that of an uneducated, ingenuous lover who probably imagined that writing was, after all, simply a question of will and application. One day, during our walk, I tried to outline for her the numerous obstacles and the not infrequent helplessness of literary creation, but I quickly perceived that she could not possibly understand me. "I'm not a writer," she said after listening to me, "nor do I have literary ambitions . . . but if I did, I think I would have so much to say . . . and in this setting, I am sure I would know how to say it well." She gave me a sidelong glance, and added playfully but seriously: "Remember that you promised to write a story in which I appear . . . now you must keep your promise." I did not respond but could not help angrily remembering the many pages covered with corrections and crossed out passages that were piling up on my desk.

I had noticed that in the morning when I sat down to work, after spending part of the night, or all of it, with my wife, I felt an almost overwhelming desire to distract myself and do nothing at all; my mind was empty, I felt a kind of lightness in the nape of the neck, a weightlessness in my limbs. Our perception of our own mental state is sometimes quite obscure. This is not true of our perception of our physical state which—especially in a man of mature age, if he is in good health—reveals itself with total clarity. It did not take long before I began to attribute my inability to work or focus my mind on a single idea, my tendency toward idleness, rightly or wrongly, to the physical emptiness I felt after our lovemaking the previous night. Sometimes I rose from my chair and stared at myself in the mirror; I recognized in the relaxed, flaccid muscles of my face, in the dark circles under my eyes and the opaque expression of the eyes themselves, and in the lassitude and languor of my posture, the absence of that energy which, in contrast, I felt every night at the moment I lay down and embraced my wife. I understood that I did not attack the page because the previous night I had spent my aggression in our embrace; I realized that what I gave to my wife I took away in equal measure from my work. This thought was not fully formulated, or at least it was not as precise as it seems now as I am expressing it; rather, it was a diffuse sensation, an insistent suspicion, almost an incipient obsession. I was beginning to believe that my creative force was seeping away each night through the body, and that in the morning there was not enough left to swell up again from the depths and refresh my mind. As one can see, my obsession took the form of images, of concrete metaphors which gave me a physical and almost scientific sense of my impotence.

Obsessions either become fixed, like an abscess, maturing slowly and eventually leading to a terrible explosion, or, in healthier cases, eventually find an appropriate expression. For several days I continued to make love to my wife at night and spend the days thinking that I could not work because I had made love to her. I must point out that this obsession in no way affected my affection for my wife or my physical transport; when we made love I forgot my fears and almost convinced myself, in that moment of desperate vigor, that I was strong enough to succeed both in love and in my work. But the following day the obsession would return, and the following night I would seek out love in order to console myself for failure in my work and recapture the ephemeral illusion of inexhaustible vigor. Finally one evening, after continuing in this vicious cycle for some time, I decided to speak of it. I was driven in part by the notion that, after all, she was the one inciting me to work, and that if she truly wanted me to write the story, as she seemed to, she would understand and accept my reasoning. When we were lying next to each other in bed, I began: "Listen, I have to tell you something I've never said before."

It was hot, and we were both naked under the covers, she on her back with her hands grasped behind her neck, her head on the pillow, as I lay next to her. She answered softly, looking at me in her usual humble, evasive manner: "Go ahead."

"This is the situation. You've said you want me to finish the story . . ."

"Of course."

"The story about you and me . . ."

"Yes."

"But as things are, I will never be able to write it."

"What do you mean, as things are?"

I hesitated for a moment and then I said: "We make love every night, isn't that so? Well, I feel that all of the energy I need for writing the story is being consumed with you. If this goes on, I will never be able to write it."

She stared at me with her enormous blue eyes which seemed dilated by the effort to comprehend what I was saying. "But how do other writers do it?"

"I don't know how they manage. . . . But I imagine that when they are writing, they are chaste."

"But what about D'Annunzio? I've heard that he had many lovers. . . . What about him?"

"I don't think he really had so many lovers. . . . He had a few famous lovers who everyone, especially he himself, spoke of. . . . But I think he was extremely measured. . . . And everyone knows that Baudelaire denied himself . . ."

She did not respond. I felt that my reasoning was almost ridiculous, but now that I had begun I could only continue. In a caressing voice, I said, "You know, I don't have to write this story, nor do I need to become a writer . . . I can give it all up very easily . . . for me, what is important is our love."

She arched her eyebrows and responded quickly: "But I want you to write. . . . I want you to become a writer."

"Why?"

"Because you are already a writer," she said, in a less certain voice, almost irritated. "I can feel that you have so much to say . . . and then you have to work at something, like everyone else . . . you can't just do nothing and be content simply to make love to me . . . you have to become someone." She groped for words, and it was clear that she did not know how to express her obstinate desire to see me do what she wanted me to.

"There is no need for me to become a writer," I answered, even though this time I felt as if I were lying, at least in part. "I am perfectly content doing nothing . . . or better yet, doing what I've done up to now: reading and enjoying, analyzing and admiring the work of others . . . and loving you. . . . And besides, if I need to do something, as you put it, I can dedicate myself to another profession, another occupation . . ."

"No, no, no," she said hurriedly, shaking her head and even her body, as if she wanted to express her denial with her entire being, "you must write . . . you must become a writer."

After this exchange, we were silent for a moment. Then she said, "If what you say is true . . . we have to make a complete change."

"What do you mean?"

"We mustn't make love until you have finished your story . . . then, when you've finished, we can begin again."

I confess that I was immediately tempted to accept this singular and slightly ridiculous proposal. My obsession was still strong and drove me to forget the selfishness at its origin. But I repressed this impulse at first and, embracing her, I said: "You love me, and this proposal of yours is the greatest proof of love that you could give me . . . but it is enough that you have proposed it . . . we must continue to make love and forget the rest."

"No, no," she said imperiously, pushing me away. "We must do this . . . now that it's been said."

"Are you offended?"

"Silvio, why would I be offended? . . . I really want you to write the story, that's all. . . . Don't be silly." And as she said this, almost as if she were trying to emphasize the affection behind her insistence, she embraced me.

We continued for awhile longer, with her insisting, imperious and inflexible, and me arguing. Finally I conceded: "All right, I'll try . . . but who knows, this may all be a mistake and I may well have no literary talent."

"That isn't true, Silvio, and you know it."

"All right then," I concluded, with difficulty. "All right . . . it will be as you say . . . but remember you were the one who proposed it."

"Of course."

There was a long pause, and then I made a gesture as if to embrace her. But she pushed me away, saying, "No, from tonight we must abstain." She laughed and, as if to soften the sourness of her refusal, took my face in her long, delicate hands, carefully, as if taking hold of a precious vase, and said, "You'll see, you'll write lovely things . . . I'm sure of it." She looked at me intently, and added, incongruously, "Do you love me?"

"What a question," I said, touched.

"Well, you will have me only when you've written the story . . . remember."

"And if I can't do it?"

"You must."

She was imperious, and this naïve, clumsy, and yet inflexible imperiousness appealed to me in the extreme. Again, I thought of the damsel who commands her knight to return with the golden fleece and kill the dragon in return for her love, but this time without rage, but rather with admiration. She knew nothing of poetry, just as the medieval damsel knew nothing of the fleece or the dragon, but for this very reason I took her command seriously. It was like a confirmation of the miraculous, providential character of creation. I suddenly felt a sense of exaltation, mixed with faith, hope, and gratitude. I moved my face close to hers, kissed her tenderly, and whispered: "I will become a writer for love of you . . . due to no merit of my own, but for love of you." She said nothing. I got up and slipped out of her room.

After that day I began to work with new faith, and soon I discovered that my calculations had not been mistaken and that, even if the connection between love and work which I had imagined did not really exist, the obsessive feeling of impotence which had oppressed me would not have dissipated if I had not taken these measures. Every morning I felt stronger, more vigorous as I sat down before the page, and—or at least so it seemed to me—more creative. And so after finding love the greatest aspiration of my life had been granted: poetry smiled upon me. Every morning I wrote ten to twelve pages in a quick, impetuous—though not disorderly or uncontrolled—flow. The rest of the day I felt overwhelmed, confused, semi-comatose, filled with the sense that aside from my work nothing in my life mattered, not even the love I felt for my wife. What followed those fervent morning hours were just the remnants, the ashes, the cinders of a glorious fire. And until the next blaze the following morning, I felt strangely inert and detached, filled with an almost morbid sense of well being, indifferent to everything around me. I realized that at this pace I would soon finish my task, perhaps sooner than I expected. I felt that I must do everything I could to harvest every last grain of this abundant and unexpected crop; nothing else mattered now. It would be both too little and too much to say that I was happy; for the first time in my life, I was living outside of myself, in an absolute and perfect world, filled with harmony and certainty. This condition made me selfish and I imagine that if during this time my wife had become sick, I would not have felt the slightest concern except for the possible interruption of my work. Not that I didn't love her; as I have said, I loved her more than ever, but it was as if she had been removed to a suspended and distant place, along with everything else that was not connected to my work. In sum, I was convinced for the first time in my life not only that I was expressing myself, which I had tried to do a thousand times without ever succeeding, but also that I was expressing myself in a perfect and complete way. In other words, I had the precise feeling—founded, as I saw it, on my experience as a man of letters—that I was composing a masterpiece.

CHAPTER VI

AFTER WORKING IN THE MORNINGS, I spent the afternoons in the usual manner, but I tried to avoid strong emotions, surprises, or distractions; on the surface I was far removed from literature, but in reality, in the recesses of my mind, I mulled over and caressed what I had written in the morning and what I planned to write the next day. Then night fell. I said good night to my wife on the landing between our two doors and went off to bed. I slept more soundly than I had ever slept, with the knowledge that I was accumulating the strength I needed for the next day's work. Upon waking, I found myself ready and well-disposed, vigorous and light, my head full of ideas that had blossomed there like grass in a field after a rainy night. I sat down at my desk and hesitated only a moment before my pen began to fly across the page as if moved by a will of its own, from one word to the next, from one line to the next, as if there were no separation or distinction between my mind and the arabesques of ink which appeared without pause on the page. In my mind there was an inexhaustible ball of yarn and by writing I was simply pulling on one end, unraveling it, and arranging the yarn on the page in elegant black patterns of words. The ball had no knots or interruptions, and it turned in my head according to the manner in which I unraveled it; I felt that the more I unraveled the more there was. As I've said, I wrote ten to twelve pages, pushing myself to physical exhaustion, mainly out of fear that this plenitude of inspiration might for some mysterious reason suddenly decrease or even disappear. Finally, when I could continue no longer, I would stand up, my legs wobbly and my head dizzy, and go over to the mirror and peer at my reflection. I could see not one but two or three reflections of myself as they slowly merged. During the leisurely, deliberate toilette that followed, I would recover my strength, even though, as I've said, I continued to feel somewhat distracted and lightheaded for the rest of the day.

Later, at the table, my appetite was vigorous and automatic, and I felt less like a man than like an empty machine that needs to refuel after many hours of frantic production. As I ate, I laughed, teased, and even composed word games, which was unlike me; I was usually serious and pensive. As on other occasions when I surrender to my own enthusiasm, there was something indiscreet and almost shameless about my exuberance; I was aware of it, but while in the past I would have been embarrassed, now I almost enjoyed it. I was there at the table, sitting across from my wife, eating; but in reality I wasn't there at all. The better part of me was still in the study, at the desk, pen in hand. I drifted through the rest of the day with the playful, somewhat disconnected, excessive attitude of a drunkard.

Had I been less enthusiastic, less inebriated by my good fortune, I would have noticed my wife's kindly attitude—the same kindly attitude I had noticed before—toward me in the whirlwind of productivity of those days. In other words, without necessarily concluding that the story I was writing was not the masterpiece I believed it to be, I might have suspected that all of this was too good to be true. Perfection is not a human quality; in most cases it belongs to the realm of lies rather than truth, whether those lies seep into our relationships with other people or they merely dominate our relationships with ourselves. This is because by sidestepping the accidents, defects, and rough edges of truth, falseness reaches its goal much more easily, without hurdles or doubts, than a scrupulous approach which hews closely to the matter at hand. As I have said, perhaps I could have been more suspicious of how smoothly my work was proceeding, after ten or more years of vain attempts. But happiness renders us not only selfish but often thoughtless and superficial as well. I told myself that meeting my wife had been the spark that had finally set off this great and productive conflagration, and I did not seek beyond this explanation.

I was so absorbed in my work that I did not pay attention to a small but bizarre incident that took place around those days. I have very delicate skin and, as they say, a "difficult" beard, resistant to shaving, which usually leaves my skin irritated and puffy. For this reason I have never been able to shave myself and have always, as I still do, used the services of a barber. Even at the villa, I managed to have a barber shave me every morning. He came from the nearby village where he owned the only barber shop, a truly modest place. He arrived by bicycle at exactly twelve-thirty, after closing his shop at noon. His arrival was the signal to stop work for the day. It coincided with the best moment of my day, with that explosion of indiscreet, physical happiness produced by my sense of accomplishment.

The barber was a short man with broad shoulders, completely bald from the forehead all the way to the nape of the neck, with a thick neck and fleshy face. His body was robust but not fat. The most remarkable feature of his face, which was of a uniformly brown, slightly yellowish color—as if he had once suffered from jaundice—were his eyes, round and large, the whites very white and characterized by a limpid, questioning, surprised, perhaps ironic expression. He had a small nose and a wide mouth with nonexistent lips, which on the rare occasions when he smiled revealed two rows of chipped, discolored teeth. His chin folded into a repulsive dimple, similar to a navel. Antonio—that was his name—had a soft, calm voice, and from the first moment I noticed that his touch was extremely light and supple. He was around forty years old and, as I discovered later, had a wife and five children. A last detail: he was not from Tuscany, but rather from Sicily, from a small town in the center of the island. As the result of a liaison during his military service, he had decided to get married and settle down in the village where he had then opened a barbershop. His wife was a farmer, but on Saturdays she left the farm and helped her husband shave the many customers who came to the shop on the eve of the feast day.

Antonio was extremely punctual. Every day at twelve-thirty, I could hear through the window the crunch of the gravel under the wheels of his bicycle in the drive below, and to me this was the signal to stop for the day. A moment later he knocked on the door to the sitting room; I rose from the desk and called out to him to come in. He opened the door and walked in, shutting the door carefully, bowing slightly and wishing me good day. The maid came in behind him, carrying a small pitcher of boiling water which she placed on a small table with wheels on which were arranged the soap, the shaving brush, and several razors. Antonio pushed the little table over to the chair where I was sitting. He took his time sharpening the knife on a leather strap with his back to me; then I saw him pour some hot water in a small basin, dip the brush in the water, and swish it around and around the surface of the soap for a long time. Finally, holding the lathery brush in the air like a torch, he turned toward me. He lathered my face for what seemed like forever, stopping only when the entire lower part of my face was covered in an enormous mass of white foam. Only then did he put down the brush and pick up the razor.

I have described these actions in great detail so as to give a sense of the deliberateness and precision of his movements. Also, I mean to give a sense of my willingness to endure, and in fact enjoy, this deliberateness and precision. Usually I do not enjoy being shaved, and the stolid meticulousness of some barbers irritates me. But with Antonio it was different. I had the feeling that the only thing that mattered was the time I spent at my desk, before his arrival. Afterwards, whether I spent my time getting a shave, or reading, or conversing with my wife, it was all the same to me. As long as this time was not devoted to my work, it didn't count, and it was indifferent to me how it was employed.

Antonio was taciturn, unlike me; after the concentration and effort of work, I felt an irresistible need to express my happiness. I talked about this and that: life in the village, the people who lived there, the harvest, his family, the local landowners, and other similar topics. One subject that interested me more than others, as I remember, was the contrast between the barber's southern background and the culture of the town where he chose to live. Nothing could be more different from Sicily than Tuscany. And in fact, more than once I encouraged him to express his curious observations about Tuscany and its inhabitants which betrayed a certain disdain and irritation. But usually Antonio responded with extreme soberness, and, as I observed, with great precision. He had a brief, reticent, sententious manner, perhaps ironic but only slightly, almost imperceptibly. Sometimes, when I began to laugh out loud at one of my own jokes or when I spoke heatedly, he would pause while applying the soap or shaving me and, with the brush or razor poised in the air, wait patiently for me to finish and recompose myself.

CHAPTER VII

I DID NOT HAVE A particular reason to speak to him in this manner; perhaps I have given the impression that I did. Even so, after some time I realized that despite all the intimate details I had drawn out of him, I had not penetrated to the core, to his true nature. Even though he was poor and had a large family, he did not seem to worry much about money. He spoke of his family with a certain detachment, with neither affection nor pride, nor any other particular feeling, as if he were speaking of something inevitable and completely natural. I quickly realized that he was not the least bit interested in politics. And though he knew his profession well and performed it gladly, he did not seem to consider it anything more than a way to get by in life. I decided finally that there was something mysterious about him, but no more so than is the case with so many common folk to whom richer people like to attribute thoughts and concerns inherent to their class, only to discover that they are preoccupied by the same things that all men hold dear.

Usually as Antonio shaved me my wife would come into the room and sit down on the windowsill in the sun with her nail file or a book. I don't know why, but her morning visits while Antonio shaved me made me particularly happy. Like Antonio, she was a mirror in which I could see the reflection of my happiness. By coming and sitting in the room in which I had done my work she helped to bring me back into the atmosphere of daily life, an indulgent, serene, orderly atmosphere that allowed me to forge ahead with my work with a feeling of security and tranquility. Every so often I interrupted my chatting with the barber to ask her how she was or what she was reading or what she had been up to. She answered without raising her eyes or interrupting her reading or pausing in filing her nails, quietly, seriously. The sun illuminated her hair, which fell in two long waves on either side of her face; behind her inclined head, through the open window, I could see the luminous trees in the garden and the blue sky. The sun brought out a tawny glimmer in the furniture, sprayed the room with the blinding glare of the reflection of Antonio's blade, and flowed benignly from the window to the furthest nooks of the room, reawakening the faded colors and dusty surfaces of the old fabrics and antique furnishings. I was so happy that on one of these mornings I thought to myself: "Until I die, I will remember this moment . . . lazing on this chair, while Antonio shaves me . . . the window open, the room filled with sunlight, and my wife sitting there, in the sun."

One day my wife came in wearing her bathrobe and told Antonio that she wanted his assistance in doing her hair. She simply wanted him to curl it; she had washed her hair that morning. She asked Antonio if he knew how to curl hair, and, receiving a positive response, invited him to come to her room when he had finished shaving me. When my wife left the room, I asked Antonio if he had ever done women's hair and he responded, not without a certain vanity, that all the girls in the area came to him. I was surprised, and he told me that these days even the most rustic farmers' wives wanted to curl their hair. "They are more demanding than city ladies," he concluded with a smile, "they're never satisfied . . . sometimes they drive me crazy." He shaved me with the usual deliberateness and precision. After he had put away his tools, he went off to my wife's room.

Once he left, I sat down in the armchair in the sun where my wife usually sat, with a book. I remember it was Tasso's *Aminta*, which I was rereading at the time. I felt particularly lucid and sensitive that day, and the enchantment of that graceful poetry, which fit so well with the luminosity and softness of the day, quickly made me lose track of time. Every so often, after a particularly harmonious verse, I would raise my eyes toward the window, repeating it in my mind; each time this gesture made me conscious once again of my happiness, just as someone who lies in a warm bed is at every slight movement reminded of its warmth. Antonio spent about three quarters of an hour with my wife. Afterwards I heard him say good-bye to the maid downstairs on the path in a calm voice, and then the crunching of the gravel under his bicycle tires as he rode away. A few minutes later, my wife returned to the sitting room.

I stood up to look at her. Antonio had covered her head in curls and had managed to transform her straight, messy hair into a kind of eighteenth-century wig. The teeming mass of curls around her long, thin face gave her a curious appearance, like a peasant woman in her Sunday best. This rustic air was further enhanced by a small bunch of fresh flowers—I think they were red geraniums—pinned just above her left temple.

"You look wonderful," I exclaimed with vehement joyfulness. "Antonio is a magician . . . Mario and Atilio in Rome should hide their faces; they are not worthy even to tie his shoelaces. . . . You look like one of the local peasant girls at the fair on Sundays . . . and those flowers are marvelous. . . . Let me look at you." As I said this, I tried to spin her around to better admire his work.

But I was surprised to see that my wife's face was darkened by some ill humor. Her sensual lower lip was trembling, a sign of anger. Finally, with a gesture of intense irritation, she pushed me away, saying: "Don't joke around, please . . . I am really in no mood for jokes."

I didn't understand, and insisted: "Oh come now, don't be embarrassed . . . I promise you that Antonio has done himself proud . . . you look wonderful . . . don't worry, you needn't feel ashamed at the Sunday fair . . . and if you go to the dance, someone will certainly ask for your hand."

As you can see, I thought that her ill humor was caused by Antonio's handiwork; I knew she was vain, and it would not have been the first time that an inept hairdresser had provoked her ire. But she pushed me away again, this time with resentment, and repeated, "I already told you I'm not in the mood for jokes."

It suddenly occurred to me that her displeasure might be caused by something other than her hair. I asked her, "What's wrong? What happened?"

She had gone over to the window and was looking out, with both hands resting on the windowsill.

Suddenly she turned around and said, "What happened is that tomorrow you must do me the favor of finding a new barber . . . I don't want that Antonio around here anymore."

I was shocked: "But why? . . . He's not a city barber, I know . . . but he's fine for me. . . . It just means that you shouldn't have him do your hair."

"Oh Silvio," she blurted out angrily, "why won't you understand me? It's not about his skill as a barber. . . . What do I care if he's a good hairdresser or not?"

"So what is it about then?"

"He was disrespectful . . . and I don't want to see him anymore. . . . Never again."

"He was disrespectful? How?"

My face and voice must have reflected the usual thoughtless indifference I felt those mornings, because she added, spitefully, "But what do you care if Antonio is disrespectful . . . you don't care at all, it's obvious."

I was afraid I had offended her, so I approached her and asked, sincerely, "Please forgive me . . . but perhaps I had not understood. . . . Tell me in what way he was disrespectful . . ."

"He was disrespectful!" She shouted with sudden anger, turning once again toward me, her nostrils fuming, her eyes hardening, "That's enough! . . . He is a horrible man . . . send him away, find someone else . . . I don't want him around anymore."

"I don't understand," I said, "he is usually exceedingly respectful . . . serious . . . a family man."

"That's right, a family man," she repeated, sarcastically, shrugging.

"Why don't you just tell me what he did to you?"

We went on arguing for a while longer as I insisted on being told what act of disrespect he had committed and she refused to give any explanation and simply repeated her accusation. Finally, after many long, furious skirmishes, I came to understand what had happened. In order to curl her hair, Antonio had been forced to stand near the chair in which she was sitting. She believed that more than once he had intentionally brushed against her shoulder and arm with his body. I repeat: this is what she believed. She herself recognized that the barber had continued working without any interruption, silently and respectfully as usual. But she swore that the contact of his body had not been accidental; she had felt his intention, his will. She was sure that by that contact, Antonio had intended to establish a rapport with her, to make a silent and unseemly proposition.

"But are you completely certain?" I asked her, astonished.

"How could I not be? Silvio, how can you doubt me?"

"But perhaps it's only an impression."

"What impression? . . . All you have to do is look at him. . . . That man is sinister . . . bald, with that neck and those eyes always looking you up and down and never looking you in the eye. . . . That man's baldness is threatening. . . . Can't you see it? . . . Are you blind?"

"It could be accidental . . . barbers have to get very close to their customers to do their work."

"No, it was no accident . . . if it had happened once, perhaps . . . but several times, constantly. . . . It was no accident. . ."

"Let's see," I said; I can't deny that I felt a certain amusement in performing such an experiment. "Sit down on this chair. . . . I'll be Antonio. Let's see."

She was boiling over with impatience and rage, but, begrudgingly, she complied and sat down on the chair. I picked up a pencil and pretended it was a curling iron and leaned forward to curl her hair. And as I had imagined, in this position the lower part of my belly was at the level of her arm and her shoulder, and I could not help touching her.

"You see," I said, "It's just as I had imagined. . . . He couldn't help it. . . . If anything, you could have leaned this way, away from him."

"That's what I did . . . but then he moved to the other side."

"Maybe he had to move over to curl your hair on that side."

"Silvio . . . is it really possible that you are so blind . . . so stupid . . . ? You seem to be doing it on purpose . . . I'm telling you, he intentionally touched me."

There was a question on my lips, but I was afraid to ask it. Finally I said: "Well, there's touching and there's *touch-*

ing. . . . Did it seem to you that when he touched you he was . . . how shall I put it . . . excited?"

She sat slumped in the armchair, biting her finger, a strange look of perplexity flashing across her angry face. "Obviously," she responded, shrugging her shoulders.

I was still unsure if I had understood correctly or if I had made myself understood. "So," I insisted, "he was clearly aroused?"

"I should say so."

Now I realized that I was perhaps even more surprised by my wife's behavior than by Antonio's. She was no longer a child, but a woman of great experience; and I was aware that in such matters, she had always displayed a certain playful cynicism. What I knew of her encouraged me to think that she would have made nothing of such an incident, or at the most, that she would have told me about it with a certain detachment and irony. Instead, she showed such anger, such hatred. I said to her, perplexed, "But, you know, this means nothing . . . it could happen to anyone to feel desire at a certain contact without meaning to, despite his best efforts . . . it has even happened to me, in a crowd or on a tram, finding myself crushed against a woman and becoming excited despite myself. . . . The mind is strong," I added jokingly, trying to calm her, "but the flesh is weak . . . damn it all . . ."

She said nothing. She seemed to be reflecting as she nibbled the tip of her finger and gazed out the window. I thought that she had calmed down a bit and so went on, still in a joking tone: "Even saints suffer temptations, let alone barbers. . . . Poor Antonio became aware, despite himself and at the moment he least expected it that you are a very beautiful and desirable woman. . . . He found himself near you and was unable to control himself. . . . It was probably as disagreeable for him as it was for you. . . . And that's the long and short of it."

She was still silent. I concluded, enthusiastically: "Ultimately, you should take this incident with a certain amount of lightheartedness . . . rather than a lack of respect, it was a kind of tribute . . . a bit rustic and coarse, I admit, but such is life."

Transported by the expansive happiness I felt after a morning's work, I had become, as you can see, deplorably facile. I suddenly realized this, and becoming more serious, I added quickly: "I'm sorry, I realize that I've been vulgar . . . but to tell you the truth I can't take this story very seriously . . . especially because I'm convinced that Antonio is innocent."

Finally, she spoke. "None of this interests me in the least," she said. "What I want to know is whether you are willing to send him packing . . . that's all."

I've said before that happiness makes us selfish. At that moment, my selfishness had probably reached its apogee. I knew that he was the only barber in the village. And I also knew that it would be impossible to find a barber in the city who would be willing to travel several miles each day to shave me. It would have meant giving up my barber and being forced to shave myself. But as I do not know how, it would have meant inflammation of the skin, scratches, cuts—in sum, a series of discomforts. And while I was working, I wanted everything to remain the same, unchanged, I did not want anything to disturb the profound serenity that, rightly or wrongly, I considered indispensable to the successful continuance of my work. Suddenly I became very serious and said, "But darling . . . you have not convinced me that Antonio was really disrespectful toward you . . . I mean intentionally so. . . . Why should I get rid of him? For what reason? Under what pretext?"

"Any pretext. . . . Tell him we're leaving."

"It's not true . . . he would know it right away."

"What do I care? As long as I don't have to see him."

"But it's just not possible . . ."

"You won't even do me this one favor," she shouted, exasperated.

"But my darling, think about it. . . . Why should I gratuitously offend a poor man who . . ."

"What do you mean 'poor man' . . . he's appalling, horrible, sinister."

"And then what would I do about my beard . . . you know very well that there are no barbers for twenty miles around."

"Shave yourself."

"But I don't know how."

"What kind of a man are you? You don't even know how to shave yourself."

"No, I don't know how. What can I do about it?"

"Let your beard grow out."

"For God's sake . . . I wouldn't be able to sleep."

She was silent for a long moment and then, in a strangled voice that was filled with a kind of desperation, she exclaimed, "So, you're not willing to do me this one favor that I ask of you . . . you just won't do it."

"But Ledina . . ."

"Yes, you won't do this for me . . . and you want to force me to see that horrible, disgusting man. . . . You want to impose his presence on me."

"But Dina . . ."

"Leave me alone." I had moved toward her and was trying to take her hand. "Leave me alone . . . I want you to send him away, do you understand?"

Finally, I decided I had to take a firm tone. "Listen, Dina," I said, "please don't insist . . . this is just a whim and I don't want to give in to whims. . . . I'll try to find out if what you say is true . . . but I will only send that man away if your accusations are proven . . . otherwise I'll do nothing of the sort."

She stared at me for a long moment and then, without a word, stood up and walked out of the room.

Once I was alone, I reflected on the incident. I was sincerely convinced that things had gone just as I said. Antonio had probably become excited on coming in contact with her arm and had not been able to hide his excitement. But I was sure that he had done nothing to facilitate or multiply the contacts which, given his task, were inevitable. In the end he was only guilty of not having been able to control his involuntary desire. And even now this is still my conviction, because I believe that certain temptations are rendered even more powerful by the fact that they are neither premeditated nor intentional.

As I thought this, alone and in complete good faith, my last pangs of remorse evaporated. I knew that ultimately I had acted out of selfishness, but this selfishness did not contradict my sense of evenhandedness. I was convinced of Antonio's innocence, and for this reason I felt no scruples in putting my comfort before what I believed to be simply a whim.

A few minutes later I saw Leda at the table. She seemed completely calm, even serene. At one point, after the maid went out with the dishes, she said, "All right . . . you can still see Antonio . . . but please make sure that I don't have to see him. . . . If I so much as meet him on the stairs, I can't answer for my actions. . . . Consider yourself warned."

Embarrassed, I pretended not to hear. She added, "Perhaps it is no more than a whim . . . but in any case, shouldn't my whims be more important to you than your own convenience?"

It was the exact reverse of what I had just thought to myself, and I couldn't help making a mental note of this fact. Luckily, the maid returned and the conversation came to an end. Later, during our daily walk, I tried to broach the subject; I felt guilty once again and would have liked to convince her of my point of view. But this time, to my surprise, she said kindly, "Let's not talk about it anymore, please, Silvio? This morning it mattered to me, I'm not even sure why, but now, after some reflection, I realize I made too much of what happened . . . I promise I don't care at all anymore . . ."

She seemed sincere and, in a way, she seemed almost to regret her earlier rage. I insisted, "Are you sure? . . ."

"I promise," she said warmly. "Why would I lie to you?"

I was silent, and we continued our stroll while conversing on other topics. And so I was convinced that my wife had put the incident out of her mind.

CHAPTER VIII

TODAY, RECOUNTING THE INCIDENT WITH Antonio, I feel I should highlight it in the context of the events that preceded and followed it. I imagine that this is the case also when one writes history. But just as in reality highly significant events pass by almost unnoticed at the time that they occur and, for example, very few people—not only bystanders but even actors involved in the event—realized that the French Revolution was the "French Revolution" when it was happening, the Antonio incident hardly registered in my imagination, even less so than these notes might lead one to imagine. I was not prepared to assign importance to this incident; my relations with my wife until then had been reasonable and happy and no one expects to find a medieval trapdoor in the center of a bright modern room. I must insist upon the innocence of my state of mind at the time; it partially excuses my selfishness and explains my superficiality. In any case, whatever my motives, I was unwilling and unable, on that occasion, to believe the worst. In fact, the following day, when Antonio tapped on the door to the drawing room at the usual time, I realized that I felt no resentment or distress. But with extreme, objective detachment, I experienced a kind of pleasure in studying this man in the light of my wife's accusations. First, while he shaved me and I spoke to him in my usual manner—and I felt no difficulty in doing so—I observed him closely. He focused on his work and executed it skillfully and nimbly as usual. I reflected that if my wife's accusations were true, it meant that he was an exceptional actor; his wide, slightly fleshy face, of a cold color between brown and yellow, seemed absorbed and placid. I could still hear my wife's words: "He is appalling, sinister, horrible," but as I observed him, I was forced to admit that there was nothing appalling, horrible, or sinister about him. If anything, he seemed paternal, imbued with an involuntary, physical authority, a man accustomed to keeping five small children at bay. Another thought occurred to me as I watched him, and even though I realized confusedly that it was silly, I latched on to it as if it were an irrefutable argument: a man as ugly as Antonio could not, unless he was mad—and Antonio was certainly not that—hope to be a seducer of women, especially not a woman like my wife, who was beautiful and who came from a completely different world. Not without a slight sense of satisfaction, I saw how fleshy his face really was, in a way that did not suggest good health. It was slightly greasy, smooth, and a bit faded, and the space between his jaw and neck seemed swollen with ill humor, reminding me of the manner in which certain tropical serpents swell in moments of excitement. He had large ears, with flat, drooping lobes; his bald head, burned by the summer sun, was brown and mottled. He seemed quite hairy, with tufts of hair sticking out of his ears and nostrils, and even his cheekbones and the tip of his nose were hairy. After unhurriedly studying his ugliness with self-satisfied care, I took advantage of a moment when Antonio turned around to clean off his razor with a piece of tissue to ask, nonchalantly, "I have always wondered whether a man like you, married with five children, has the time or the desire to pursue other women."

He responded without smiling, as he again turned toward me, razor in hand. "There is always time for that, Mr. Baldeschi."

I admit that I had expected a different answer and felt almost a sense of shock. "But isn't your wife jealous?" I objected.

"All wives are jealous."

"So you cheat on your wife?"

He held up the razor and, looking squarely at me, said, "Excuse me, Mr. Baldeschi, but that is my business."

I felt myself turn red. I had asked this indiscreet question because I believed, foolishly, that I had the right, as a superior, to do so; but he had put me, as they say, in my place, on an equal footing, and this was something I had not expected. I had a slight feeling of irritation and was tempted to say, "It is also my business, given that you had the impudence to bother my wife." But I repressed the impulse and said, somewhat mystified, "You mustn't take it badly, Antonio . . . I was just making conversation."

"I know," he said, and as he moved the razor down my cheek, shaving me slowly, he added, as if to temper the brusqueness of his first answer and relieve my embarrassment, "You see, Mr. Baldeschi, we all love women . . . even the priest here near San Lorenzo has a woman who has borne him two children. . . . If we could peer inside people's heads we would see that everyone has a woman somewhere . . . but no one is eager to talk about it, because if they did, it would get around and trouble would come of it. . . . As we know, women only trust men who are discreet."

I listened to his lesson regarding the value of secrecy in amorous affairs, but I still doubted whether he belonged to the class of men who can be discreet and are trusted by women. That morning, I spoke no more of the matter, and changed the subject. But I wondered for the first time whether, after all, my wife's accusation might be true. That afternoon Angelo, the sharecropper's son, arrived to go over the accounts as he did once a week. I sat with him in the drawing room, and after finishing the accounts I mentioned Antonio, asking him if knew the barber and what he thought of him. The young, fair-haired farmer, with an air that seemed both shrewd and thick at the same time, responded with a faintly malevolent smile, "Yes, we know him . . . of course we know him."

"It seems to me, or am I mistaken, that you don't much like him."

After a momentary hesitation, "There's no doubt he's a good barber . . ."

"But . . ."

"But he's not from around here, and as we know, foreigners are different from us. . . . Maybe where he comes from things are different . . . but around here, no one can stand him, that's for sure."

"Why is that?"

"Oh, lots of reasons." Angelo smiled again, shaking his head, an embarrassed and malicious smile, filled with dislike for Antonio, imbued with the knowledge that whatever complaint the local inhabitants had against the barber had its comic side.

"Give me an example," I insisted.

He became serious and answered me in a grave tone that struck me as a bit ingratiating. "Well you see, Mr. Baldeschi, first of all, he's a skirt-chaser . . ."

"Really?"

"And how . . . you have no idea . . . beautiful, ugly, old, young, it's all the same to him . . . and not just in his shop when they go to have their hair curled . . . but anywhere . . . ask anyone. . . . On Sundays he rides his bicycle around the countryside . . . as if he were out hunting . . . it's indecent. . . . But let me tell you, one day someone will put an end to it." Now that he had cast aside his usual reserve, Angelo became effusive, basking in his stolid, flattering moralism, like a country bumpkin trying to please his master.

I interrupted him with a question: "What about his wife?"

"Poor woman, what can she do? . . . She cries, she despairs. . . . He taught her how to shave the customers and sometimes he leaves her to run the shop and goes off on his bicycle. He tells her he's going to town, but instead, he rides around looking for girls. Just imagine, last year . . ."

At that point, I realized that Angelo had given me all the information I needed and that now I would hear a litany of gossip about Antonio's bad behavior. It seemed undignified to encourage him or listen to his story, so I changed the subject, and shortly thereafter sent him away.

When I was alone again, I fell into a kind of distracted reverie. So, my wife was right, or at least there was a good chance of it. So, this Antonio was a libertine, and it was quite possible that he had attempted to seduce my wife. Now I realized that this mysterious Antonio, who did not seem particularly passionate about his work, or loving toward his family, or interested in politics, was no mystery at all. Antonio was a third-rate Casanova, a mundane erotomaniac. And his unctuous, circumspect manner was that of a man who, as he had put it, was popular with women because he was discreet.

I had a strange feeling of disillusionment. Ultimately, almost involuntarily, I had hoped that Antonio would not deflate so quickly and so easily in my mind. Now I realized that I had enjoyed the fact that there was something slightly mysterious about him. Now that the mystery was gone, he was just a poor wretch who ran after women, all women, including, perhaps, those who, like my wife, were completely out of his reach. Before I came to this realization, if I had allowed myself to be influenced by Leda's antipathy, I might have grown to hate him. But now that I knew more about him I felt only a kind of compassion mixed with contempt, a feeling that was humiliating both for him and for me; I felt reduced to a mortifying rivalry with this small-town Don Juan.

But even now, strange as it may sound, I was still convinced that he had not really dared to lay hands on my wife and that, as I had suspected from the first, he had been moved, against his own better judgment, to manifest his admiration for her in the only way he knew. The fact that he was a libertine did not in my opinion contradict this suspicion; in fact, I thought it helped to explain the facility with which he had become excited by the first fortuitous contact. Such alacrity is comprehensible in an adolescent, whose senses are always at bay, but less likely in an experienced, unflappable man of forty. Only a libertine who is in the habit of cultivating certain instincts and only those could have such a ready and irresistible sensibility.

I imagined that perhaps he had not been overly upset to find himself in this embarrassing situation and that he had simultaneously encouraged and attempted to resist it. But it still seemed beyond a doubt that it had all begun as an accident, not an act of will.

It is possible that this initial inclination to believe Antonio innocent—though I still believe him to be so—was derived at least in part from my own egotism, or from the fear of being forced to fire him and shave myself. But even if this was the case, I was certainly not aware of it. I looked on the entire episode with extreme objectivity, and in fact objectivity—or the overlooking of the connections between things and subjective motivations—is one of the most effective forms of deception. Had I even conceived the possibility of feeling jealousy, my conviction that Antonio was innocent and the feeling of contemptuous commiseration that I now had for him, as well as my wife's excessive reaction, had abolished any reason for jealousy from the very beginning. I am not a jealous man, or at least I do not believe myself to be so. Every passion I feel is corroded by the acid of reflection; this is simply my way of dominating my passions, by simultaneously destroying their dominion over my senses and the suffering that they cause.

After the conversation with Angelo, I went for my usual walk with my wife. And for the first time I had the very precise feeling that I was deceiving her. I felt that I should have told her what I had found out about Antonio, but I didn't want to because I realized that it would have simply reignited her fury, possibly even more strongly than before, just when it seemed to have quieted down. Uncertain and filled with remorse, I finally said at a moment when she seemed distracted, "Perhaps you are still thinking about Antonio's insolence. . . . If you really want me to, I'll send him away."

If she had asked me at that moment, I think I would have given in to her. My selfishness had been shaken, and I needed only a slight encouragement to give her satisfaction. She shuddered, "The barber? No, I wasn't thinking of him at all . . . to tell you the truth, I'd almost forgotten the whole thing."

"But if you want me to, I'll send him away," I insisted, encouraged by her seemingly sincere indifference, sensing that my proposal would be rejected.

"I don't want you to," she said, "I don't care . . . it's as if nothing had happened at all."

"But I thought . . ."

"Now it is something that concerns you and only you," she concluded with a pensive air, "in the sense that only you know whether or not you are disturbed by his presence."

"To tell you the truth, he doesn't bother me."

"So why should you send him away?"

I found her reasonableness pleasing, even though I became aware once again of a slight feeling of disappointment. But inevitably the happiness caused by the final realization of my creative instinct kept me from paying more attention to any of the sensations that I was beginning to feel. The next day Antonio returned, and I was surprised to note that his curious allure, far from being dissipated by Angelo's stories, had remained intact. In fact the mystery I had sensed when I knew nothing about him persisted even now that I thought I knew everything. This mystery had simply been transferred to a more inaccessible place, that was all. It was, as I now realize, a bit like the mystery of all things, great and small: everything can be explained but existence itself.

CHAPTER IX

IN THE DAYS THAT FOLLOWED I continued to work with a momentum and facility that seemed to increase as I approached completion. Antonio came every morning and, once the initial embarrassment passed, I continued to study him with my original curiosity. I felt that there was now a bond between us; I could have broken it from the start by firing him as my wife had suggested, but I had not done so and for this reason a new connection, tacit but undeniable, had been born between us. It is difficult for me to describe what exactly my feelings were regarding this connection. Originally, the relation between us had been that of a superior and an inferior, but after my wife's accusation this relation had been modified. The superior had become a deceived husband or a husband who might believe himself to be deceived, while the inferior had become the deceiver or could at least believe himself to be so. Both of these relationships were utterly conventional; the first was based on the putative dependence and authority conferred by payment and receipt of wages, and the second on the equally fictional moral obligation imposed by the bonds of matrimony. By suggesting that I replace Antonio, my wife had in fact suggested that I accept these two conventions without taking into account the effective and particular facts of the situation. I had refused her suggestion and Antonio had not been replaced. Now I felt that because of my refusal a new relation had been born between us which was certainly much more real, because it was based on the situation as it actually was and not as it should have been. But this relation was not classifiable or definable and as such was open to all possible outcomes. I understood that by refusing to behave as another person would have in my place, in other words as a superior and as a husband, I had opened the door to all possibilities, because everything now depended on developments in the actual situation in which we found ourselves that were not determined by any convention. I realized that the attitude that my wife had suggested, as conventional as it was, was the only way to give the current situation a recognizable physiognomy. Without this attitude, anything was possible, and the situation dissolved into an indistinguishable mess. My wife's solution would have allowed each of us to keep to a recognized, fixed role; outside of it our roles became confused, foggy, and interchangeable. These thoughts underlined the utility of moral rules and social conventions, superficial as they are; they are necessary in order to fix and create order in the natural disorder of things. On the other hand, I thought that once these rules and social conventions had been laid aside, the disorder must settle down and reorder itself on the basis of an absolute need. In other words, if one excluded the solution proposed by my wife there must be another that would be dictated by the actual nature of things. Like a river which can be channeled by artificial dykes or can be allowed to flow according to the inclination and topography of the terrain, in both cases—though of course with different results—the river will form a stream along which it will flow toward the sea. But this second solution, which was the most natural and the most dependent on fate, could come far in the future and might never come to be; Antonio would continue to shave me, I would finish my work, and then my wife and I would leave. I would never know what truth there had been in my wife's accusations. Today I can explain my thoughts in an orderly and lucid manner, but in those days, these thoughts were but vague sensations, as though an uncomfortable knowledge had emerged where once there was only comfort and a lack of awareness.

Some will be surprised that I could think or feel such things as the situation was unfolding before my eyes and as I saw that my dearest affections were threatened or seemed to be so. But I repeat what I have already said: I was creating something, or at least so I believed, and everything else was secondary. Of course I had not ceased loving my wife or caring about my honor, but artistic creation had by some strange miracle lifted the weight of necessity from these things and transferred it instead onto the pages of the book I was writing. If, instead of accusing Antonio of having treated her with disrespect, my wife had revealed that she had seen him clean his razor with a page from my story, I would certainly not have speculated about his ignorance or his irresponsibility; I would have fired him on the spot. And yet such an action would have been more comprehensible, justifiable, and forgivable than the one he stood accused of. What was it that rendered me indifferent to his behavior toward my wife and instead violently susceptible should he touch my work? Here lies the mystery which Angelo had done nothing to illuminate and which in reality lay less with him than with me. It is a mystery that, one could say, emerges and will always emerge each time one goes beneath the surface of things.

Meanwhile, my wife no longer came to see me as she used to while Antonio was shaving me, and I believe that, until the barber left the house, she stayed in her room. Her attitude irritated me because it revealed that she still held firmly to her conventional reaction and had no intention of changing it for a reasonable and speculative attitude like my own. I don't remember exactly when or where I asked her why she no longer came to see me in the mornings. She answered immediately, with only the slightest hint of impatience: "But Silvio . . . sometimes I doubt your intelligence. . . . How can you expect me to come to see you? That man has not been punished for his insolence . . . if I came in he might think that I had forgiven him, or worse. . . . By not appearing I make it clear that I have made a decision to avoid a row and not mention what occurred that day to you."

I don't know what mischievous demon led me to answer, "Perhaps he thought you hadn't noticed. . . . This is worse . . . you show him that you did notice and yet you do nothing about it and do not ask me to do anything about it."

"The only correct thing to do," she responded calmly, "would have been to send him away that same day."

CHAPTER X

FINALLY ON ONE OF THOSE mornings, I wrote the last word of the last line on the last page, and I closed the notebook containing my story. I felt as though I had made a huge effort and had been working for an extremely long time, but in reality I had scribbled down the equivalent of about a hundred printed pages and had worked for a little over twenty days. With the notebook in my hand, I walked over to the window and leafed through the pages involuntarily; tears came to my eyes, and I did not know if they were tears of joy or exhaustion. I could not help thinking that this stack of pages contained the best part of my life, everything I should live for from now on, and everything I had lived for up to that moment. I leafed through the pages slowly and as I looked at them I felt my eyes blurring and tears falling on my hands. Then I saw Antonio cross the gravel driveway on his bicycle, and I quickly put the notebook away on the desk and dried my eyes.

Later, when Antonio had left, I went to my bedroom, and as I dressed, I continued to think about my work, as I did everyday. On other days I had reflected only on the pages I had written that same morning, but that day, for the first time, my memory considered and caressed the entire story, from beginning to end. This thing which I referred to in my mind as my masterpiece lay before me, complete and perfect, and I could finally take pleasure in its wholeness as one enjoys a landscape after a long and arduous climb during which one has only been able to glimpse fragmentary views of the landscape. In reality, these sensations can only be suggested, not described. I'll just say that while I reflected on my story, time seemed suspended in a kind of rapture, and in fact it was. Suddenly the door opened, and my wife peered in: "What are you doing? Lunch is served . . . it's been on the table for three quarters of an hour."

I was sitting on the bed in my bathrobe, and my clothes were still on the chair where I had left them. I looked at my watch; Antonio had left at approximately twelve forty-five. It was now two o'clock. I had been sitting there on the bed for an hour and a quarter, with one sock on and the other in my hand. "Forgive me," I said, shuddering violently, "I don't know what happened . . . I'm coming." I dressed hurriedly and met her downstairs.

In the afternoon, after my first excitement had subsided, I began to pose the first questions. I had decided to read the story to my wife as soon as I finished it. I trusted her more than myself or any critic. As I have said, she was not highly cultivated, nor was she involved in literary circles, and her interest in books was similar to that of most people who are more interested in plot than in style. But for this very reason, because I knew that she would judge the story just as most readers would, I trusted her. I knew she was quick and intelligent enough, filled with good sense, incapable of lying to herself even for reasons different from those of professional literati. Her judgment, as I saw it, would not strictly be a measure of the literary value of the story, but it would allow me to understand whether or not the book had life. After all, the first question to answer about any book is whether it is alive as a whole. There are terribly flawed books—poorly constructed, muddled, disorderly—that are alive, and we read them and always will; and there are books that are perfect in every way, well-constructed, well-composed, orderly and polished, which we put down despite all their perfections, and that we don't know what to do with. I had developed this conviction after many years of reading and critical writing. Therefore, the first thing I needed to know about my book was whether it was alive, and no one could tell me this better than my wife.

I approached this appraisal, which to me seemed like the ultimate test, with complete serenity. I still had many doubts about the literary value of my story, given that I had not yet reread it and had the feeling that it had been written in haste. I asked myself: As I had progressed in writing, had I not shed the discouraging feelings of sterility, difficulty, inadequacy, vagueness, and sophistry that had tormented me my entire life and had stopped me each time I attempted to write? Had I not felt, as I wrote, a kind of diaphragm ripping open in my chest, allowing its contents to flow out, not in a thin stream, but gushing and spreading outward like a flood? Had I not in fact felt all the time that my very being was reflected faithfully in what I was writing, and that the words I was writing were reflected in me? These and other notions had reassured me of the effect that these pages would have upon my wife.

A few practical difficulties remained. The manuscript was not a complete mess, but it contained a fair number of corrections and additions between the lines which would have rendered a reading difficult and unpleasant. I would probably be forced to stop and study the page in order to recapture a forgotten logic, thus destroying the uninterrupted and complete spell I wished to create. It was also possible that in the fervor of this first draft I might have missed some particulars, some finishing touches. That afternoon as I walked with Leda and we talked about this and that, I debated the pros and cons of reading the story to her that evening. Finally, I decided it was best to postpone my reading for about ten days, during which I would type up the manuscript. I realized that as I copied the story, many things that were out of place could be corrected, and others that were missing could be added. The style would be tightened, and I would be able to eliminate every ill-expressed thought. Furthermore—and this was the decisive argument—I would be able to enjoy my masterpiece for ten days longer in the intimate form of an unread manuscript. This last thought convinced me to wait.

I had brought my typewriter with me from Rome; it was new, or almost new, as I had only used it to write a few business letters and the odd article. It was an American model, the newest on the market, and during my periods of sterility the awareness of its excellence filled me with bitterness. In those days I thought of myself as one of those rich, incapable writers who have everything they could ever desire to compose their masterpiece—money, time, a large, quiet study, embossed writing paper, expensive fountain pens, the latest typewriter—except the genius. Such writers bow their heads before the humble, inexpensive notepad on which a threadbare adolescent scribbles in pencil as the inspiration strikes him, a few lines here and there in the back of a café or shop. But now, the feeling of sterility brought on by the gleaming typewriter and the other commodities I had at my fingertips had disappeared. I was rich and idle, but I had created something. The lives of men who create, or who believe themselves to do so, are filled with these kinds of superstitions.

But that afternoon, when I went to check if the typewriter was in working order, I discovered that I had left my typing paper in Rome. I knew there was no chance that I would find this paper in the village, and I decided to go to the nearby city to buy it. There was a stationery store there that supplied all the offices in the district. But it was too late to go that same day, since the sharecropper's gig, the only form of transportation at my disposal, had left in the morning. I decided to go on the following day. That evening I told my wife that I had to go to the city to do some shopping, without specifying exactly what I meant to buy; I asked her pro forma whether she would like to accompany me. I say pro forma because I knew that the gig was small and that she did not enjoy riding in the slow, uncomfortable carriage. I was quite happy to go alone;

I was so contented that solitude seemed preferable to company. As I had predicted, she declined, without making any comment about the reason for the trip. After a moment she asked, "What time will you be home?"

"Early . . . in any case by lunch."

She was silent, and then asked, "What should I do if the barber comes?"

I reflected for a moment, and then answered, "I will certainly arrive before he does . . . but in case I am delayed, have him wait for me." I had no desire to go to a barber in the city, where the instruments are reused again and again on many customers. Antonio did not bring his own instruments; I supplied everything he needed.

She said nothing and we changed the subject. Now that I had finished my work I felt that I loved her just as much as before and perhaps even more. Or rather, I had loved her all the time, but during those twenty days I had suspended the expression of my love. We were sitting at the table in the small dining room. Leda, as usual, was wearing an evening dress; it was elegant and white, falling straight down to the floor, cut low in the back, draped simply like a Greek peplus. Her neck, fingers, and earlobes were decorated with large, costly jewels. A lamp with a parchment lampshade, set in the middle of the table, illuminated her face with a soft, golden light. Her face was carefully made up and she had kept the short, curly hairstyle from the day that Antonio had combed her hair. For the first time I realized that now that her long, narrow face was no longer framed by the loose, flowing tresses, it had taken on a new aspect; her face looked younger, less poignant, and now it was imbued with a kind of cruel, classical sensuality. No longer caressed and softened by the wave of her hair, the still, intense slant of her enormous blue eyes, the nervousness of her pointed nose, and the smiling fleshiness of her mouth were revealed. She seemed exposed and yet more real, with a satyr-like, archaic air that reminded one of primitive Greek sculptures, which from the front offer an ambiguous ironic expression, and from the side a goat-like Semitic profile. This impression was increased by the small bunch of red flowers that she had pinned in her golden hair above the temple, as on the day of the incident with Antonio. . . . As I gazed at her, I said, "You know that Antonio's hairstyle suits you after all? I hadn't realized it before."

She seemed to shudder almost imperceptibly at the sound of the barber's name, and lowered her eyes. With her long fingers, she played with the large glass bottle stopper, and between her long, pointed, scarlet-colored fingernails—the color of rubies—in the light of the lamp, the multifaceted stopper looked like an enormous diamond pierced with brilliant rays of light. She said slowly, "The idea of doing my hair in this way was not Antonio's but mine. . . . He only executed it, and poorly at that."

"And how did it occur to you?"

"I used to wear my hair this way years ago when I was a girl," she said. "It's a style that suits very young girls, or," and she smiled slightly, "mature women, like me."

"What do you mean 'mature,' don't be silly . . . those flowers look lovely."

The maid came in and we were silent as we served ourselves. Then, as soon as the maid had left again, I put down my knife and fork and said, "You look like someone else . . . or rather yourself, but in a completely new way." Suddenly I felt very agitated and I added, softly, "Leda, you are very beautiful . . . sometimes I may forget it, but then a moment comes when I realize that I am desperately in love with you."

She was eating and did not respond, but I could see there was no disdain in her, but rather a calm satisfaction that was visible in the slight trembling of her nostrils and the fold of her lowered eyelids. It was her way of accepting compliments that pleased her, and I knew it. I was overwhelmed by a wave of love. I put my hand on hers and murmured, "Kiss me."

She raised her eyes, looked at me, and asked simply, perhaps without irony, "Is your work finished?"

I lied. "No, but I cannot look at you without loving you and wanting to kiss you . . . my work be damned."

As I said this I took her arm and drew her toward me, and she leaned over toward me in her seat. She resisted, arching her eyebrows, with a tempted and semi-serious air, and said, in an amorous tone, "You're crazy," and, turning toward me quickly, she gave me the kiss I had asked for, with a sudden, sincere impetus. We kissed hurriedly and passionately, pressing our lips against each other forcefully, like two innocently ardent adolescents who are not yet experienced at love and who spoil their enjoyment with nervousness and impatience. And with this fleeting kiss, which I had not merely plucked but stolen from my wife's lips, I, too, felt that I was again an adolescent boy, afraid of being observed by a mother's severe eyes rather than by those of a devoted elderly maid, filled with embarrassed complicity. After the kiss, we composed ourselves, like two children; she was calm and serene, and I was still slightly out of breath. The maid did not return, and I looked at my wife and felt the desire to laugh, and did so, tapping her hand with my own. She asked suspiciously, "Why are you laughing?"

"I'm sorry . . . I'm not laughing at you . . . I'm laughing because I'm happy."

She asked me, in a calm, conversational voice, looking down as she ate, "And why are you so happy?"

This time I could not resist and said candidly: "For the first time in my life, I have everything I desire, and, what is even more precious, I am aware of it."

"What do you desire?"

"For years and years I wanted to love a woman and to be loved by her. And here we are, I love you and believe that you love me as well. . . . For years and years I aspired to write something lasting, alive, poetic . . . and today I finished my story and can say that I have accomplished this as well."

I had not meant to mention the story to my wife until I finished typing it. But my joy was so powerful that I was unable to resist. Her reaction to the news surprised me, even though I knew she loved me and took an intense interest in my life. "You've finished!" she exclaimed with a joy that was flattering in its sincerity, "You've finished," and her voice echoed with a clearness that enthralled me. "Oh Silvio, you hadn't said anything."

"I didn't tell you because even if I've finished in the real sense, I still need to type up the manuscript . . . I will be truly done when I've finished typing it."

"It doesn't matter," she said with her flattering, absolute spontaneity, "you've finished and this is a great day. . . . We must toast your book!"

She was sweetly and impetuously affectionate, and her blue eyes, so beautiful and luminous, gazed at me seductively, as if seeking to caress me. With a slightly trembling hand, I poured wine in our glasses, and then we raised them over the table. "To your health and to your book," she said softly, gazing at me. I drank and watched her drink and then she put her glass down and leaned toward me, offering her lips, and this time we truly kissed, passionately and for a long time, and only after the kiss did we notice that the maid was in the room watching us as she leaned against the credenza, tray in hand.

"Anna, you too must drink. This is a great day," my wife said in the confident and elegantly natural tone with which she was able to resolve even the most embarrassing situations. "Silvio, pour Anna a glass . . . Anna, you must drink to Signor Silvio's health." At first the old woman squirmed, giggling, but finally she said, "Well, if it's to Signor Silvio's health . . ." She placed the tray on the credenza, took the glass, raised it in a clumsy toast, and drank. With the same naturalness, my wife served herself and began to eat, meanwhile asking me affectionate, direct questions about my work: "And this time do you feel sure that you've written something worthwhile?"

"Yes, as far as one can be sure about such a thing . . . but I am a better judge than some, since I'm also a good critic. . . . At least of this I am certain."

"You know, I must tell you I'm very happy," she said after a brief silence, putting her hand on mine and looking into my eyes. I raised her hand to my lips and kissed it. I was infinitely grateful to my wife for the manner in which she had taken the news of the conclusion of my work; like a touchstone, it revealed once again the pure gold of her feelings for me. In addition I felt inebriated by her joy, as if her reaction had come not from someone who was uneducated and unprepared but from a critic with the highest credentials. I believe that even the most knowing writers experience this juvenile sensation at least once in their lives, early in their careers, when they timidly and hopefully face the judgment of their closest and most longtime colleague. Relieved by this joyous reaction, I realized that we had already finished eating, left the table, and moved to the sitting room, where my wife was standing before me, serving coffee.

I don't remember much about that evening, as we forget the faces of people and their expressions after lightning illuminates everyone with its blinding light. I can only remember that I was excited, cheerful, exalted, and that I spoke of my future and hers. I also explained to her how it had occurred to me to write a story based on the two of us and our marriage, describing the material I had used and the variations and considerations I had introduced. I cited other famous books, making comparisons; I listed literary precedents and linked my work to a tradition. At times I interrupted myself to make tangential references or tell stories. Finally, I picked up a book, an anthology that had recently been published, and read some poems by contemporary authors out loud. My wife was sitting on the couch, beautiful and elegant, her legs crossed and her foot, in a silver shoe, hovering in midair, as she smoked and listened, and I realized that she was following my voice with the same affection, truly as untarnishable as gold, that she had displayed spontaneously when I announced that I had finished the story. Alone in that nineteenth-century sitting room, sitting among the old, creaky furnishings, in that isolated villa among the fields, we enjoyed—or at least I enjoyed—a few hours of the most incomparable intimacy. Then, precisely when I closed the book, the lights went off.

It was not unusual for the electricity to be cut off; it was the time of the olive harvest, and the current was often diverted to the olive presses. I walked through the darkness toward the French window that gave onto the gravel drive and opened it wide. The gravel was bathed in white light from the moon, and beyond the dark frame of the trees, the full moon filled the nocturnal sky with a silver hue. I stood on the step looking for the moon. Then, as I turned, I saw it rising quickly behind the mountain from which rose the old city; at first it was no more than a sliver, and then, as if driven by an irresistible movement, it became larger and rounder until finally it was a complete, dense globe surrounded by bright light in a luminous sky. Its rays fell straight down on the brown walls of the city, putting them in cold, solitary, porous relief. The light seemed to imbue the walls with an air of excited expectation and vigilant watchfulness as in the days when they had defended the city. I lost myself as I stood there looking at the moon suspended above the walls. I heard my wife's voice from the sofa where she sat, "It must be time to go to bed, don't you think? It must be very late."

Perhaps this was simply an invitation to sleep. But in my exaltation I took it for an amorous call, and I quickly came back inside, saying, "There's a magnificent moon. . . . Why don't we go for a walk?" I observed my wife as she followed me in silence, walking toward me from the darkness of the sitting room, and I was gratified by her docility. We stepped out together onto the gravel path.

The air was filled with the profound quiet of autumn nights when the summer insects have gone silent until the following year. The two plaster dogs that guarded the house at the edge of the drive also seemed to add to this quiet, with their vivid, almost affectionate attitudes, in stark contrast to their mute whiteness. We took the front path, passing through the low arch formed by the trees. As soon as we entered the dense shadows, I put my arm around Leda's waist and felt her body slacken indolently, elegantly, without sentimentality, as if responding to an anticipated gesture. Thus intertwined we began to stroll down the path, between two rows of inclined trees; the moon shimmered through the clumps of undergrowth, mottling the tree trunks and foliage here and there with an ambiguous, white glow. We walked the length of the path and when we had almost reached the gate, we took another path, between two rows of cypress trees. Beyond the trunks of the trees we could glimpse the illuminated, silent fields, and, at the end of the path, in the empty, silvery air, we could make out another expanse of countryside. My wife leaned on my arm and I could feel, under her dress, the soft fold where her upper body met the roundness of her hip. At the end of the path we turned onto a narrow trail that separated the garden from the fields. The garden came to a natural end in the open countryside, and the branches of the last trees arched beyond the trail, over rows of vines. A bit higher up, on a small knoll, stood the sharecropper's farmhouse; we could already see its rustic façade, vividly illuminated by the moon. The trail that ran alongside the garden passed beneath the farmhouse and around the base of an elevation on which stood the threshing floor and three haystacks, and then meandered into the countryside, where it disappeared. We walked slowly, with the trees of the garden on one side and the grassy slope of the knoll on the other. We passed the farmhouse and the area below the threshing floor, and I looked up toward the three haystacks; one, made with fresh, pale yellow hay, was intact; another was brown, made with older hay; and the third was almost gone—only a slender segment remained, in the shape of a rudder, against the misshapen pole that held it upright. The moon illuminated and delineated the massive structures against the dark, empty background of the countryside, and seemed to isolate the three haystacks on the knoll. They looked carefully positioned, and that, along with their monumental quality, made one forget their real nature and suggested some mysterious significance. I could not help but think of the groups of enormous stones set in circles by Druids here and there on the planes of France and England. I told my wife that those three haystacks, placed in the light of the full moon, reminded me of the dolmen of Brittany, and began to describe the pagan rituals performed there in prehistoric times. An idea had occurred to me, or rather a desire: to climb up the hill and possess her there, on the hay, on the bare earth, under the light of the moon. In this manner and in these ideal surroundings, I wanted to solemnize both the conclusion of my work and the resumption of our conjugal love. I cannot deny that this desire belied some literary notions, but so be it: as an intellectual, it was appropriate that for me literature merged with the most profound and most concrete impulses. I truly desired Leda and the idea of making love to her there, outside, under the full moon, seemed the most natural thing in the world, and this idea could easily have occurred to a man more simple and less cultivated than myself.

CHAPTER XI

I TOLD HER THAT I wanted to climb up the knoll to gaze upon the vast panorama one could see from there; she accepted and, still arm in arm, we climbed up the steep slope on the slippery grass. When we reached the top, we stood still for a moment while we looked out at the landscape. We could see the entire plain stretching before us in the clear night, and in that vast pullulating expanse, the moon revealed rows of trees, hedges, the empty spaces of fields, and vineyards. Here and there the light of the moon paused on the façade of a farmhouse, bathing it in silver. Along the horizon, the earth was separated from the sky by a row of black mountains. A distant rumbling, perhaps a train hidden beyond the fields, echoed in the sleeping countryside, confirming its vastness and silence.

My wife gazed at the landscape, almost in awe, as if she were trying to penetrate the secret of its serenity and silence; I again put my arm around her waist, and began whispering to her, pointing out particular objects on the plain and exalting the beauty of the night. Still whispering, I turned her so that she faced the hill behind us, and pointed out the walls of the city at its summit. We had moved closer to one of the haystacks; there was hay spread out on the ground, and during the day the sharecropper's children played there. Suddenly I embraced her, whispering, "Leda . . . isn't it more lovely here than in your room?" As I said this I tried to pull her down toward the ground.

She looked at me, her luminous blue eyes dilated by a sudden temptation. Then, pushing me away, she said "No, the hay is dirty . . . and all those sharp points . . . I'll ruin my dress."

"What does it matter?"

"Your work isn't yet complete," she said quickly, with an unexpected, flirtatious laugh. "When you've really finished, we'll return here at night . . . all right?"

"No, that's not good enough. The moon won't be out. It must be tonight."

She spoke softly, still seemingly unsure of herself: "Let go, Silvio," and then, in a moment, she shook free and ran away, down the hill, still laughing. Her laugh was fresh and girlish, filled with an affectionate nervousness that trembled with the temptation I had read in her eyes; it almost compensated for her rejection. Perhaps it was better that things had ended this way, I reflected, with a tender rejection and a graceful laugh. She ran ahead of me, down the path between the garden and the vineyard, but I caught up with her easily and took her in my arms. Now I felt that her laugh had satisfied my desire, and after kissing her, I continued to walk beside her, grasping her hand in mine. The light of the moon created two separate shadows, joined by the hand, which preceded us; the chastity of our return seemed more amorous than the embrace that had eluded me on the hill. We walked down the path and reached the gravel clearing in front of the house. Meanwhile the electricity had returned and the French windows of the sitting room were illuminated and welcoming. We went in and walked straight up to the second floor. She walked in front of me and she had never seemed so beautiful to me as she did in that soft, elegant motion that underlined the sensuous lines of her body. On the landing she again said, in a teasing, sensual manner, "Finish your work . . . and then we'll go back to the threshing floor together." I kissed her hand and went to my room. Moments later, I was asleep.

When I awoke the following morning, my feeling of exaltation had not dissipated and had perhaps grown to its highest point. My wife was still sleeping when I hopped aboard Angelo's gig and headed for the city. Angelo, perhaps thinking it was his duty to do so, began to describe the situation of the farms in the area, and I let him prattle on without paying much attention, lost in my thoughts, or rather my impressions. The carriage rolled down the lane, upon which the first rays of the morning sun were already playfully shimmering, then alongside the old wall, and finally joined the main road. The day had the balmy, soft gleaming feel of fall; I looked around at the farmland, already somewhat naked and languid, on which even the faintest variations in color and the smallest particulars were visible to the eye in that even light, so different from the devouring glare of summer, and I could not get enough of looking at everything around me. Now it was a red leaf that fell from a vine in a tiny whisper of breeze; there it was an ever-changing pattern of soft light and shade on an old brown, green, and gray wall. Further along, a lark flew up from the road almost under the horse's hooves, punctuating the space with its bursts of flight, and finally resting near a clod of dirt in a barren field; the earth had just been turned up and still bore the polish of the spade's edge. There were toxic-blue verdigris stains on the white walls of the farmhouses. And there the moss, yellow as gold, grew on the darkened tiles of the roof of a small church that resembled a granary. There were large, pale green acorns visible among the darker leaves of a young oak that rose up from a field next to the road. I took pleasure in these and other similar, minute details as if they had been filled with an ineffable significance, and I knew that this new, all-embracing receptiveness was a product of my happiness, which was also ineffable and new.

After we had gone some distance along a plain, the road began to rise softly but continuously up the side of a hill. The horse slowed to a canter. For the first time I looked closely at the old walls built at the summit of the hill; they were brown, but the edges were illuminated by the radiance of the sun, and I suddenly felt invaded by an uncontrollable exaltation, as if those walls had been the objective, finally visible, not just of that morning's brief outing but of my entire life. The gig ascended slowly and for a moment, as I looked up at the walls, I saw myself not as I was—a knot of confused, fleeting perceptions and feelings—but fixed in time, cloaked in the predestined and mysteriously simple aura that history attributes to its heroes. The great, encouraging men that I admired had ridden under this same sun, on mornings like this one, along similar roads, just as I was at that moment; this realization seemed like a confirmation that perhaps I was about to become one of these men. I felt it in the intensity of the moment as I was living it; this seemed like the clearest sign of my admission to the realm of greatness and eternity. I caught myself repeating: "October twenty-seventh, nineteen hundred and thirty-seven," several times, to the harsh, sustained, regular rhythm of the horse's hooves as it climbed the hill, with the sense that the fascinating quality of that date, articulated in each of its syllables, already suggested a kind of premonition.

Meanwhile, one step at a time, we had arrived at the doorway to the city, built out of enormous Etruscan masonry and surmounted by a slender medieval arch. It was gilded by the sun as farmers driving mules or carrying baskets passed through it ahead of us, and it was truly a morning like any other, on that hilltop as everywhere else. After we passed through the gate, my exaltation suddenly flagged as the gig climbed the paving stones of a steep street, between two rows of old houses. We reached the main square; I dismounted, directing Angelo to meet me there in an hour, and I went off to buy the paper. The shop I had in mind was a bit higher up, on the Corso, and I did not have much difficulty finding it. But I was surprised to discover that the paper store did not carry typing paper but only oversized printer's sheets. Somewhat irritated, I resigned myself to buying a hundred of these double-sized sheets, with the idea that I would cut them each in half. Carrying the roll of paper under my arm, I went into the main café and drank a vermouth, standing at the bar; it was an old café, dark and dusty, with a few dubious-looking bottles on the shelves and no customers on the banquettes that lined the walls. I left the café, returned to the square, crossed over to the newsstand, and after gazing for a long time at four or five illustrated magazines and humor papers, I bought the morning newspaper and sat down on the stone bench in front of the town hall under the curlicued coats of arms of families long since extinct and the iron rings for hitching horses. I regretted having told Angelo to return an hour later, but consoled myself with the thought that Angelo had things to do and that I would have been forced to wait for him in any case. Half of the asymmetric, narrow square surrounded by medieval palazzi was in the shade—the other half was bathed in bright sunlight, and because it was not market day, the square was deserted. In the hour or so I waited there I did not see more than a dozen people walk by, and at least half of them were priests. I read the entire newspaper and realized that I was not at all unhappy to wait, since my work was complete and it was too late to start typing the manuscript that day. I felt calm and was in my usual mood; when I finished the paper, I began to observe the activities of the many artisans whose workshops were located around the square. The sun was rising in the sky and the severe shadow of the town hall became smaller as it retreated across the paving stones. Somewhere a bell—perhaps from a convent—began to toll stridently; it was followed by the deeper resonance of the bells of the main church. It was noon and the entire town seemed to reawaken, and several groups of people entered the square. I got up and slowly walked the entire length of the Corso to the public gardens, a sunny meeting place where I thought I might find Angelo. And in fact there I found him, conversing with some farmers. We returned to the carriage for our descent.

During the return trip, perhaps due to fatigue, my thoughts settled into a less excited rhythm. I remember that I began to think about the publisher I would like for my book, about the cover that I might choose, about the critics and what they might write, about who might like the book and who might not. Then I thought about Leda and I reflected on how lucky I had been to find her, and perhaps for the first time since our wedding, the fragility of our bond surfaced in my mind. I was almost frightened by the thought that my entire life depended on her feelings for me and on mine for her, and that everything could change and I might lose her. At this thought, I became agitated and anxious; I understood, as I struggled to catch my breath and felt my heart tremble, how bound I was now to Leda and how I could no longer live without her. I realized that, because she belonged to me, I felt so fulfilled that I sometimes thought that I was capable of living without her; but as soon as I imagined being separated from her, I understood that alone I was the most deficient, the most wretched, the most derelict of men. And I realized that this separation could occur at any moment. I suddenly felt annihilated, traversed from head to toe by a cold shiver, even beneath that burning sun; my eyes swelled with tears and I realized I had gone pale. Almost hysterical, I commanded Angelo to drive the horse to go faster: "For heaven's sake," I cried out angrily, "shall we not try to make it back before nightfall?" Luckily we had reached the level plain, and the horse, sensing our proximity, took off at a rapid trot. I anxiously monitored the road with the ardent desire to reach home and Leda as soon as possible, hoping to find Leda just as I had left her. Here is the first stretch of the main road in the open countryside, I thought, and here is the next, after the bridge, and here is the final stretch, along the wall surrounding our property. Here is the gate, and here is the lane. The gravel drive was filled with sunlight, and standing on the threshold of the French window, as if she had been standing there for years, an almost unbelievable sight after such terror, was Leda, dressed in pale hues, with a book in her hands. Joyfully, I noted her expectant pose from far away; she must have been reading in the sitting room with the window open, and at the sound of the wheels of the gig on the gravel, she had come out to see my arrival. The gig came to a stop and I jumped off, greeted her, and went in.

"It's late," she said, following me, "the barber has been here for some time . . . he's waiting upstairs."

"What time is it?" I asked.

"After one o'clock!"

"It's Angelo's fault," I said, "I'll go now and have my shave and I'll be right down."

She said nothing and stepped out into the garden. I climbed the stairs four at a time and went into the sitting room.

Antonio was waiting, standing near the little table on which the razors were laid out. He greeted me, bowing slightly. I said, breathlessly, "Hurry, Antonio, it's very late . . . try to be quick," and I flung myself down on the armchair.

I realized that part of the reason I felt so rushed was that I was hungry. That morning I had only consumed a cup of coffee; my stomach was empty and my head was spinning, and this hunger made me irritable. My irritability became apparent immediately, as Antonio, in his usual leisurely way, began to unfold the towel and tie it around my neck. "Why doesn't he hurry up?" I thought to myself, "I told him I was in a rush . . . damn it all." The composure of his movements, which I usually enjoyed, now seemed unbearable. I wanted to tell him to hurry but as I had already done so, I did not want to repeat myself and so became even more irritated. When he turned to lather up the brush, I watched him impatiently, counting the seconds. My appetite and impatience increased.

After he had worked up a good froth, Antonio turned, brush in hand, and began to spread lather on my face. He was a master at creating an enormous, dense white mass of froth on his customers' faces. But that morning I was irritated by his bravura. Each time he swirled the brush I thought it was the last stroke, but I was mistaken: catching a tuft of foam that was about to fall with the tip of his brush, he continued with the same steady motion, whipping up the soapy lather. For some reason the idea of sitting there with all that foam on my face made me feel ridiculous, and worse yet, I felt almost as if Antonio was consciously trying to make me feel foolish. This suspicion was absurd, and I rejected it immediately, but it is a good indication of how my hunger had upset my mood. Finally, seeing that there was no end to this process, I cried out angrily, "I told you to hurry, and instead you take forever even to apply the soap!" I saw Antonio shoot me a quick glance with his round, light, surprised eyes; wordlessly, he placed the brush in a bowl and picked up the razor.

But before turning again, and after I had spoken, he could not stop himself from whipping the froth on my right cheek one last time. I took his disobedience to be almost a gesture of insolence, and my irritation grew even greater.

He sharpened the razor quickly on the strap and then leaned over and began to shave me. With his usual light touch and skill, he removed most of the foam from my right cheek, and then leaned over to begin shaving the left side. As he did so he leaned against my arm and for the first time I noticed this contact, and could not help being reminded of Leda's accusations. There was no doubt. As he leaned over me he pressed his body against my arm and shoulder and at this contact I felt an extreme repulsion. I could feel the softness of his lower abdomen, which I imagined to be hairy, muscular, and sweaty, wrapped in undergarments of dubious cleanliness; suddenly, through my own feeling of distaste, I could understand my wife's. It was a particular kind of distaste, inspired by a careless and sensual contact, which, despite its casual nature, cannot but arouse the suspicion that it was voluntary.

I waited a moment, hoping that he would move away. But he did not and could not, and suddenly my repulsion became stronger than my prudence. I moved away brusquely. Immediately, I felt the cold of the razor cutting into my cheek.

At that moment, with no explanation, I was filled with a wave of fury at Antonio. He had immediately held up the razor and was looking at me with surprise. I jumped up, holding my hand to my cheek, which was already beginning to bleed, crying out: "What are you doing? Are you crazy?"

"But Signor Baldeschi," he said, "you moved . . . so abruptly. . . ."

"I did not," I screamed.

"Signor Baldeschi," he insisted, almost supplicating, with the respectfully aggrieved self-control of our social inferiors when they know themselves to be in the right. "Why would I cut you if you hadn't moved? Believe me, you moved . . . but it's nothing, hold on." He went over to the table, uncorked a small bottle, took a wad of cotton-wool from a package, and poured some of the alcohol on the cotton-wool.

Mad with fury, I yelled, "What do you mean it's nothing? . . . It's a huge cut!" and, tearing the cotton out of his hand, I went over to the mirror. The burning sensation of the alcohol pushed my exasperation to the limit. "It's nothing!" I yelled, angrily throwing away the bloodstained cotton wool. "Antonio, you don't know what you're talking about . . . listen, it's better if you leave."

"But Signor Baldeschi . . . I haven't finished . . ."

"Forget it. . . . Leave and don't come back," I yelled. "I don't want to see you again, do you understand me?"

"But Signor Baldeschi . . ."

"Enough! Leave now and I don't want to see you again around here . . . ever again. . . . Do you understand?"

"Should I come back tomorrow?"

"Not tomorrow or any other day. . . . Enough!" I yelled as I stood in the middle of the room, with the towel still tied around my neck. He bowed slightly, almost ironically, and said, "As you like." He walked to the door and disappeared.

Alone in the room, my anger died down. I removed the towel, wiped away what little lather was left on my face, and looked at myself in the mirror. Antonio had cut me when he was almost finished, and except for the long red cut, my face looked fine. I dipped some cotton-wool in alcohol and carefully disinfected the cut. Meanwhile, I reflected on the strange manner in which I had lost my temper and driven Antonio away; I realized that the cut was simply a pretext. The truth was I had wanted to fire him all along, and had done so at the first opportunity. But I knew that I had done so only when it could no longer inconvenience me, in other words, after I had finished writing. I realized that I would not be able to present my actions to Leda as an homage to her wishes, because, just as I had kept him on, despite her accusations, for selfish reasons, now I had rid myself of him for the same selfish reasons. At this thought I felt some regret, and for the first time I understood that, perhaps without realizing it, I had not behaved honorably toward my wife. Meanwhile I dressed, and as soon as I was ready, went down to the ground floor.

She was already sitting at the table. We sat in silence for some time, and then I said: "You know, I sent Antonio away . . . for good."

She did not look up: "And now how will you shave?"

"I'll try to do it myself," I answered, "and it will just be for a few days, because we'll be leaving soon, won't we? I don't know what got into him today, but he cut my face, made this long gash here . . . do you see it?"

She raised her eyes and studied the wound. She asked anxiously, "Did you disinfect it?"

"Yes, and you know, the cut was just a pretext . . . the truth is I couldn't stand him any longer . . . you were right."

"What do you mean?"

I realized I could only tell her what Angelo had told me if I pretended he had just done so today. So I lied: "This morning Angelo and I talked about Antonio. . . . He told me that Antonio is an unrestrained libertine . . . apparently he's infamous in the area . . . he bothers all the women. . . . So I realized you might have been right . . . even if in your case it's not clear that he acted intentionally . . . and so I took advantage of the cut to get rid of him."

She said nothing. I continued, "It's strange, nevertheless. . . . One would never guess it . . . I can't imagine what women see in him: he's bald, yellow-skinned, fat, short . . . hardly an Adonis."

"Did you find the paper you needed in the city?" she asked.

"Not exactly . . . but I found printer's sheets. They will have to do." I understood that the subject of Antonio made her uncomfortable and I was happy to speak of something else, just as she had. "Today I will begin copying my book. I want to work in the afternoon and evening—that way I shall finish more quickly."

She said nothing and continued to eat calmly. I spoke of my book and of my plans, and then said, "I will dedicate this book to you, because without your love I would never have written it," and I took her hand. She looked up and smiled. The expression of kindliness that I sometimes perceived in her attitude toward me was so patently written on her face that even a blind man could have seen it. I sat there, disconcerted, with her hand in mine, my enthusiasm frozen within me. She was smiling at me the way a mother smiles at a child who runs toward her breathlessly at an inconvenient moment to tell her; "When I grow up I want to be a General!"

Then she said, "And what dedication will you write?"

In my mind, I translated her question: "And what kind of general will you be?" I answered self-consciously, "Oh, something simple. . . . 'To Leda,' or perhaps, 'To my wife,' why do you ask? Would you prefer something longer?"

"Oh no, I didn't mean anything in particular."

She was a million miles away. I pulled my hand away and fell into a pensive silence as I looked out of the window at the trees in the garden. I thought that one of us should break the silence, but nothing happened. She said nothing, and her silence seemed definitive, as if she were lost in her own thoughts and had no desire, or so it seemed, to emerge from them. To hide my disappointment, I tried to appear jovial: "You know what one writer said? 'To my wife, without whose absence this book would never have been written . . .' "

She smiled faintly and I quickly added, "But our case is the exact opposite . . . without your presence I would never have been able to write it."

This time she did not even smile. I could no longer restrain myself, and blurted out, "But if you don't want me to, I won't write anything at all."

My voice must have expressed a clear bitterness because she seemed to make an effort to focus her thoughts, and again taking my hand she said, "Oh Silvio, how can you think it doesn't make me happy?" But even now, the kindliness in her attitude was clear. It was just like a mother to a child who has said, "But if you don't want me to become a general, I won't," and to whom the mother responds, "Oh no, I do want you to become a general. And I want you to win many battles." I understood that it meant nothing, and the irritation I had felt earlier toward Antonio, which I had attributed to hunger, returned. I rose up from the table abruptly, saying, "I think Anna has brought out the coffee."

CHAPTER XII

LATER SHE WENT UPSTAIRS TO rest, and I returned to the sitting room to begin copying my manuscript. I placed the typewriter on the desk, opened it, and put the cover on the floor. I placed the manuscript to the right of the typewriter, and to the left I put the blank pages and the carbon paper. I took three sheets of paper, inserted two pieces of carbon paper between them, placed them in the typewriter, and typed the title. But I had not centered the pages, and as I soon discovered, the letters were all on one side of the page. I had also forgotten to write the title in capital letters. So I removed the three sheets and replaced them with three new ones. This time the title was in the middle but, when I checked, I realized the carbon paper was facing the wrong way and the title had not been copied onto the other sheets. I impatiently tore these sheets out of the typewriter and again replaced them with three new pages. This time I made several errors, rendering the title illegible. Suddenly I felt almost afraid. I stood up from the desk and began to walk around the room, peering at the old German prints on the walls: *The Castle at Kammersee*, *Panorama of the City of Weimar*, *Storm over Lake Starnberg*, *The Rhine*

Waterfalls. The house was immersed in a profound silence, the shutters were half-closed, and the room was filled with a wan light that invited sleep. I realized that I was tired, and that perhaps it was not a good idea to begin this task under these conditions; I laid down on a stiff couch in the darkest corner of the room.

I stretched my hand toward a small end table covered with knickknacks next to the couch and picked up a gilt-edged sketchbook bound in red leather. It was an old keepsake from 1860. On each page, the owner had sketched a landscape in pen; the landscapes were quite similar, in their unschooled style, to the prints I had just been observing. Beneath each landscape, in an English script, were written thoughts and opinions in French. I looked at the landscapes one by one and read many of those sentimental, conventional reflections. I was feeling drowsy. I returned the sketchbook to the table and fell asleep.

I slept for about an hour, and every so often I woke up and saw the desk, the chair, the typewriter, and thought to myself that I should be working, and experienced a bitter feeling of impotence. Finally, as if at a signal, I awoke completely and jumped to my feet.

The sitting room was dark; I walked to the window and threw open the shutters. The sky was still luminous but the sun had become oblique and entered the room at a slant. My mind empty, I sat down at the desk and began to type.

I typed mechanically, and after the third page I stopped and fell into a profound reflection. I wasn't really thinking about anything in particular; it was just that I couldn't seem to capture the sense of the words that I had written so feverishly just a few days earlier. I could see that they were parts of speech, but they seemed to be no more than that and they had no weight, no meaning. They were words but not things, vocabulary words as they appear lined up on the pages of a dictionary, words and nothing else. At that moment my wife peered into the sitting room to ask if I wanted to have tea. I accepted the invitation with a sense of relief, happy to be distracted from the sense of detachment and absurdity that I had felt as I went through my manuscript, and I followed her downstairs. My wife was already dressed for our daily stroll, and tea was on the table. I made an effort to shake myself, and began to converse with her in a self-possessed manner as we drank our tea. My wife seemed less distracted and preoccupied than before, and this improved my mood. After tea, we went outside and began to walk down the path toward the front gate.

As I have said, there were not many directions to choose from, and so we took the path we knew so well, through the fields. I walked ahead, and Leda followed. I realized immediately that my thoughts had remained fixed in that distracted, uncomprehending state that I had experienced while sitting before my manuscript, but I made an effort, only partially successful, to push this preoccupation out of my mind and converse lightly on insubstantial topics. The path meandered, its shape determined by the fields between the farmhouses. Every so often it passed by a threshing floor near a farmhouse, and then continued on between two hedges or along a ditch next to an orchard or the last row of vines in a vineyard. In the diffuse, clear, sparkling autumnal light, the plain was visible all the way to the horizon, from field to field, from crop to crop, flat and luminous, with a few trees here and there, dark against the backdrop of the serene sky, each leaf illuminated by the sun. When I came to a small humpbacked bridge across an irrigation ditch I stopped and looked out at the countryside, and my wife walked ahead. I remember she was wearing a simple grey dress with red, green, yellow, and blue spots. When I looked at her from behind I was frightened by the thought that she, like my manuscript, seemed to be only a sign in space. "Leda," I said softly, and I felt as if what I had said had absolutely no meaning. Then I said to myself, "My name is Silvio Baldeschi and I am married to a woman called Leda," and it seemed as if I had said nothing at all. Suddenly it occurred to me that the only way I could escape from this feeling of irreality was to inflict or experience pain, for example by pulling my wife's hair, throwing her down on the sharp gravel of the path, and receiving a kick in the shins in return. And similarly, perhaps the only way to appreciate the value of my manuscript was to rip it to shreds and throw it into the fire.

I felt I was going mad; it seemed that it was not possible to comprehend one's own existence or that of others except through pain. But I found some consolation in the thought that if this was true, if not only my manuscript but also my own wife, whom I knew I loved, was incomprehensible to me, then this feeling of absurdity was not related to the quality of my work but to myself.

My wife was looking for a place to sit down, a difficult task in this intensely cultivated landscape, where each plant had its purpose, each clump of earth its seed. Finally we peered down toward a trench at the bottom of which flowed a small brook known as the "S," perhaps because of its tortuous course. At that point the two grassy banks sloped down gently and the brook formed a small rounded pool of dense, greenish water, in the shade of three or four poplars. A sloping slab of cement, half on the bank and half submerged, was used by the local women to beat and wring the laundry, transforming this apparently solitary spot into a busy washroom. As she let herself fall back on the grass, my wife said that in that farmland, every corner was put to use, and so it was.

We began to speak softly in the fading light and murmur that precedes nightfall. My wife had pulled out a blade of grass and was chewing on it; sitting just below her, I watched the blurred shadows of the poplars reflected on the surface of the water. We talked for a while about that spot and about the rest of the day, and then, with the slightest pretext—I asked her if she wanted to go to the mountains that winter. She began to tell a story from her past, about something that had happened two years earlier in a mountain town. Her first marriage had, as I have said before, quickly come to an end, and then for the subsequent ten years she had lived alone and I knew that she had had many lovers. I felt no jealousy toward these men who had preceded me, and she, seeing my indifference, had begun, at first prudently and then more openly, to tell me about them. Why she did this I am not sure; perhaps it was vanity, or perhaps, now that her life was so different, she did so out of a sense of nostalgia for her past freedom. I cannot say that I enjoyed these stories; when I least expected it, I felt a slight shudder, like the involuntary reflex of a sensibility I did not know myself to possess. It was not quite jealousy, but neither did I feel the complete, rational objectivity on which I prided myself. But that day, while she chewed on her blade of grass, her eyes open wide and staring fixedly not at me but perhaps at something she could see in her mind's eye, she recounted one of her affairs, and as she did so I realized that this time the slight uneasiness provoked by her evocation of the past was actually a pleasurable feeling, like smelling salts for a person who has fainted. When we sat down I had felt threatened by an uncomfortable sense of irreality, and now her warm, sensual voice was telling me about real things, which had really happened, and furthermore which had happened to her and were unpleasant for me. Another, more sanguine person might have felt his blood boil in a fury of hatred, but for me, bloodless as I felt, they brought back a sense of who I was and of who she was to me. Of course I suffered as I heard her tell me in great detail how she had been approached by a man who pleased her, how she had allowed him to kiss her, how they had slept together; but this suffering, which was sufficient to reawaken my languishing vitality, was almost pleasurable, and thus lost its destructive, useless quality. It was perhaps a poison, but one of those poisons that in small doses can bring a sick man back to life. She told me about an affair she had had with a red-haired lieutenant in the Alpine troops: "I was vacationing in the mountains in March and as there was little snow, I climbed up to a chalet at six thousand feet. There was never anyone up there, and I spent the days out in front of the chalet, in a folding chair, reading in the sun. One day a group of Alpine soldiers arrived from the valley. I was in my chair as usual, and they began to take off their skis around me to go for a drink in the chalet. Among them was a young officer with red hair, covered in freckles, with blue eyes. He was wearing neither a hat nor a jacket, and as he leaned over to undo his skis in his grayish-green tunic, I saw that his back was robust and young, strong but slender at the waist. As he raised his head he looked at me, I looked at him, and that was it. I was afraid he had not understood me when in fact he had understood perfectly, as you will see. I remember that I got up anxiously and went into the dining room of the chalet. He planted his skis in the snow and came in after me. His companions were already sitting at a table and he sat down with them, his back to the window, facing the dining room. I went to the counter and ordered some tea and sat down at the table in front of him. They joked and laughed, and like a madwoman, I sought out his eyes with my own. Later he said that he had noticed my maneuvering, but at the time, seeing that he did not even deign to look over at me, I was convinced he had not. Finally he looked over, and, in order to put all doubts to rest, I brought my fingers to my lips and blew him a kiss, like a young girl. He saw this but made no move in response, and I feared that he was not attracted to me. Pretending to feel uncomfortably warm, I removed my jacket and, fiddling with a strap under my shirt, I slightly bared one shoulder. Soon after, I got fed up and went back out to the folding chair in front of the chalet. They remained there for a while, drinking, and then they came out, took their skis, and went off. I remained in my chair, waiting, still unsure. The sun went down and I continued to wait, numb, almost without hope. Just when I had lost all hope, he reappeared over the slope on his skis. I went to meet him, and he said, 'I had to invent lies . . . they didn't believe me, but there it is.' That is what he said, as if we had always known each other. I said nothing; I was so stirred that I did not even have the strength to speak. He removed his skis very slowly, and I took him by the hand and led him directly to my room on the second floor. Imagine, I never even found out his name."

I've transcribed the story just as she told it, in her words, brief and grave. She never lingered over the sensual details in these stories of hers, but seemed to suggest them by the rich tone of her voice and by a kind of acrid, carnal expression in her entire person. She became animated and more beautiful. And on that day, when she finished telling her story, I began to understand that she had a vitality which was stronger than any moral rule and that I needed to come in contact with even if it meant repressing certain reactions in myself. For a moment I was not a husband listening in a perturbed state of mind to his wife's amorous reminiscences but a clod of dried earth in danger of crumbling to dust that had finally received a much-needed rainfall. I gazed at her as she chewed on her blade of grass, absorbed in her thoughts, and I realized with wonder that I was no longer tormented by my earlier feeling of irreality.

CHAPTER XIII

SLOWLY, WE RETURNED TO THE house, and, calm and happy as ever, I joked and talked familiarly. When we reached the house it was later than usual, and my wife went straight up to change for dinner. I put a record on the gramophone, a Mozart quartet, and sat down in an armchair. I was in a light, cheerful mood. When the minuet began, with its ceremonial, sentimental back and forth, expressed as strong, sonorous questions followed by plaintive, graceful responses, it occurred to me that these questions and responses belied something deeper than male and female characteristics; they were two well-defined attitudes, one active and the other passive, one aggressive and the other tentative, one flattering and the other flattered. I reflected that the notes suggested an inalterable relationship through time, and that it made no difference if the two dancers existed in the present or two centuries ago. It could have been the two of us, my wife and I, dancing this dance in our own way, just as before us, throughout the ages, countless couples had danced it. Lost in these thoughts, the time passed, and I was almost surprised to see Leda appear before me in the same low-cut dress she had worn the night before. She turned off the gramophone halfway through the quartet, saying with a slight hint of impatience, "I don't know why, but I don't feel like listening to music." Then she sat next to me, on the armrest of the chair, and asked in a casual voice, "So, will you begin copying your story tonight?"

As she asked this question, she looked at her reflection in a pocket mirror and adjusted the fresh flowers in her hair. I responded in a satisfied tone, "Yes, tonight I will begin, and I will work until at least midnight . . . I want to get a good start and finish in a few days."

Adjusting her hair, she said, "Until midnight? Won't you be sleepy?"

"Why?" I asked. "I'm accustomed to working at night . . . and," I concluded, putting my arm around her waist, "I want to finish quickly so I can turn my attention completely to you."

She put the mirror back in her bag and asked, "Why? Do you think we're not together enough?"

I answered, allusively, "Not in the way I would like."

"Oh, I see what you mean." She got up and began to pace back and forth in the sitting room with impatient, insistent footsteps. I asked her if something was bothering her.

"I'm hungry, that's what's bothering me," she said with a certain hardness and irritation, adding, more mildly, "Aren't you?"

"Not very, and I don't want to eat too much because otherwise I'll get sleepy."

"What restraint you have," she said, and I shuddered because it was said in a disagreeable tone which I had been unprepared for. "What do you mean?" I asked gently.

She realized I was offended and caressed me as she stood before me, saying, "Forgive me . . . hunger makes people aggressive . . . don't pay me any mind."

"It's true," I said, remembering the incident with Antonio, "hunger makes us irritable."

"On a different subject," she said quickly, "do you like this dress?"

Perhaps she was merely changing the subject; as I said, she had worn it the previous evening and I had already seen it on several occasions. Still, I said, indulgently, "Yes, it's beautiful and you look lovely in it . . . please turn around for me."

She turned compliantly so I could see her, and then I noticed a slight change. The previous evening, beneath the light, almost transparent material I had noticed around her stomach and hips the outline of an elastic silk and rubber girdle, made in the United States, which she sometimes wore to contain her silhouette. I did not like this girdle; not only was it visible, but it was tense and hard to the touch beneath the thin veil of the dress and had an almost repugnant orthopedic air. As I noted, on this evening she was not wearing the girdle, and in fact she appeared more supple and slightly heavier. "I see you're not wearing your American girdle tonight," I said casually.

She looked at me and answered, indifferently, "I didn't wear it because it is uncomfortable. . . . How can you tell?"

"Because I noticed you wore it yesterday."

She did not respond, and at that moment the maid came in to tell us that dinner was ready. We went into the dining room, sat down at the table, and my wife served herself. I noticed that, contrary to what she had said, she did not seem to be hungry at all; she took only half a spoonful of food from the serving platter. As I served myself, I said, "You said you were hungry, and now you're hardly eating."

She looked at me with an unhappy air, irritated that I had noted the contradiction. She said, "I was wrong . . . actually, I'm not hungry at all . . . in fact, I feel slightly nauseous."

I asked her worriedly, "You don't feel well?"

She hesitated and then responded, very quietly, "No, I think I'm all right . . . but I'm not hungry." I noticed that her voice was weak and when she paused she seemed to be out of breath. She was silent and played with her food, then she lay down the fork and sighed deeply, holding her hand to her chest. I was alarmed. "You don't feel well," I said.

This time she conceded. "Yes. . . . I feel a bit weak," she said in a feeble voice, as if she were about to faint.

"Do you want to sit down on the couch?"

"No."

"Do you want me to call the maid?"

"No, but would you give me a drink?"

I poured some wine in her glass, and she drank it and looked better. The maid brought in fruit, but Leda did not touch it; I ate a bunch of grapes, slowly, as she watched me, seeming to count each grape I put in my mouth. As soon as the grape stalk fell from my fingers, she rose up brusquely and said, "I'm going to bed."

"Are you sure you don't want coffee?" I asked, alarmed by her loud, unhappy voice and followed her into the sitting room.

"No, no coffee, I want to sleep." She was standing near the door with her hand on the handle, rigid and impatient.

I asked the maid to bring my coffee to the sitting room on the second floor, and followed her; she had opened the door and was walking toward the stairs. I reached her and said casually, "I'm going to work now."

"And I'm going to sleep," she said without turning back.

"But are you sure you don't have a fever?" I asked, trying to touch her forehead. She shielded herself and then said impatiently, "Silvio, with you one always has to be so explicit . . . I don't feel well and that's it."

I fell silent, embarrassed. On the landing I took her hand as if to kiss it, but I hesitated and said, "I want to ask a favor."

"What favor?" she asked with a catch in her voice that surprised me.

Awkwardly, I said, "I would like you to come in to my study for a moment and kiss the first page of the story . . . it will bring me luck."

She laughed affectionately and with some strain; but both the affection and the effort seemed strangely sincere. She rushed into the sitting room exclaiming, "How superstitious you are . . . how silly . . . but I'll do as you wish."

I turned on the light, but she had already reached the desk in the dark. "Which page is it? . . . Tell me which page I should kiss," she repeated with hurried zeal.

I approached and handed her the page on which I had typed the title: "Conjugal Love." She took it, read the title out loud and made a face which I did not understand, and then she brought the page to her mouth and pressed her lips against it. "Are you happy now?"

Beneath the title the paper bore the trace of her lips, two red semicircles like flower petals. I looked at her for some time, gratified, and then I said gently, "Thank you, my darling."

She quickly caressed my cheek and then went toward the door saying hurriedly, "Good luck with your work . . . I'm going to bed . . . I am really very tired . . . please don't wake me for any reason . . . I want to sleep. . . . See you tomorrow."

"See you tomorrow."

She left, almost crashing into the maid who was bringing in the coffee. After the maid had gone, I lit a cigarette and sat down at my desk, drank two cups of coffee, and finally uncovered the typewriter. I felt completely lucid, as if my mind, instead of being filled with the usual vague, dense tangle of casual and contradictory reflections, was instead dominated by a clean, precise machine, in perfect working order: like a scale or a clock. It seemed to me that this mechanism excluded all vanity, pride, fear, or ambition. It was a very precise instrument, incorruptible and neutral, with which I was preparing to calibrate, evaluate, and perfect my work as I copied it. With my cigarette between my lips and my eyes on the paper, I began to type, continuing the page which I had begun earlier.

I typed about four lines and placed the cigarette in the ashtray, pushed away the typewriter, picked up the manuscript, and began to read it. I have said that I felt exceptionally lucid; just now, copying those four lines, I had sensed a note of falseness, different and yet very reminiscent of the sound made by a cracked glass. Let me speak clearly: the thought flashed through my mind that the story might not only *not* be a masterpiece but actually be deficient. As I've pointed out before, I have considerable literary experience, and in certain circumstances I can be a capable critic. I realized now that I felt with the help of this extraordinary and aggressive clarity of mind all my critical abilities were being applied to the page. The words were no longer words but fragments of metal that I was testing with absolute precision aided by the touchstone of my taste. I did not read the complete story because I did not want to be fooled by the rhythm of the narrative, and instead I read a line here and there; the more I read, the more worried I became. It seemed that there was no longer any doubt: the story was truly deficient, irreparably so. Suddenly, overtaken by a mania of almost scientific objectivity, I took a piece of blank paper, picked up my fountain pen, and began to jot down my observations as they came to me, as I did while reading a book I was planning to review.

At the top of the page I wrote in a steady hand, "Observations on 'Conjugal Love,' by Silvio Baldeschi." I drew a line and began to jot down my notes. I followed the method I used when composing my critical pieces, analyzing all the various aspects of the work and waiting until the end to coalesce these specific observations in a single, complete judgment. Naturally, I was not planning to write an article about myself, but rather in a way to document this first inkling that the story was deficient, and perhaps also to punish myself for having believed it to be a masterpiece. But above all I was trying to achieve some sort of definitive clarity regarding my literary ambitions.

CHAPTER XIV

THIS IS WHAT I WROTE on the first page. First: Style. And beneath that, hastily: clean, correct, decorous but never original, never personal, never new. Generic, expansive when it should be brief, brief when it should be expansive, ultimately superfluous because it is the result of effort. A style without personality, reflecting a diligent composition in which there is no vibrancy of poetic emotion. Second: Plasticity. None. Says things instead of showing them, writes instead of depicting them. Lacks distinctness, volume, concreteness. Third: Characters. Worthless. It's clear they were not created through sympathetic intuition but rather studiously copied and transcribed with the aid of a defective instrument, a vacillating, foggy, embryonic judgment. They are mosaics made out of minute, empty observations, not free, living creatures. They meander, contradict themselves, at times they disappear from the page, leaving only their names; and these names, Paolo or Lorenzo or Elisa or Maria, belie their unreality because one feels that they could be switched with little effect. They are not characters but blurry photographs. Fourth: Psychological truthfulness. Lacking. Excessive casuistry, excessive subtlety, too many asides, and not enough good sense. Psychologism and not psychology. It is clear that the author moves from the outside inward at random, not down the main road of truth but through the alleyways of sophism. Fifth: Feeling. Cold and shrunken, concealed by exaggerations, outbursts, and flights of fancy that betray emptiness and ambition. Sixth: Plot. Poorly constructed, unbalanced, full of inconsistencies, expedients, patches, and tricks beneath an apparent effectiveness and polish. Abundance of deus ex machina and interventions by the author. Everything managed from the periphery, mechanically, because the center lacks a motor. Seventh and final point: Total evaluation. The book of a dilettante, of a person equipped with intelligence, culture, and taste but completely lacking in creative power. The book reveals neither an original idea nor a new sensibility. It is written on the backs of other books, a second- or third-class artifact, a hothouse flower. Practical conclusion: can it be published? Yes, surely, it could be published, perhaps in a luxury edition, with one or two lithographs of tasteful paintings, and it could even, with the appropriate publicity in the literary world, achieve what is usually known as critical success, in other words, several reviews, even good ones, determined by the level of indebtedness and friendship toward the author. *But the book doesn't count.* I underlined this last sentence, which brought together all my thoughts, reflected for a moment, and then added the following postscript: it is clear that the book was written in a state of perfect and impetuous happiness and is therefore the best that can be expected from the writer, who was, in fact, convinced as he wrote it that he was creating a masterpiece. It follows then that the writer expressed himself in this book as he is: a man without a creative sense, weak, deliberate, and sterile. This book is a faithful mirror of the man.

I was done. I placed the manuscript in its sleeve, removed the pages from the typewriter and closed the cover. Then I got up, lit a cigarette, and began to pace back and forth in the sitting room. I realized that this insight, which had pleased me so much earlier, had now transformed itself into the false lucidity of a feverish, desperate delirium. After having forced myself to write this severe judgment of my own work, this lucidity stayed in my mind like the moonlight on the surface of a roiling sea on which float the large and small pieces of a shipwreck. Lucidly, feverishly, my thoughts circled around the definitive devastation of my ambitions, illuminating it from all angles, in other words rendering it even more bitter and complete. During those twenty days when I had done nothing but write and had closed my mind to all other worries, it seemed that an enormous mass of disappointment had accumulated in a hidden corner of my consciousness. Now that the walls of my irrational presumptuousness had been destroyed, this disappointment rushed in all directions, and despite my lucidity I felt overwhelmed by it. I discarded the cigarette I had only just lit, and almost without realizing it, I pressed my temples with my hands. I realized that the failure of my book overshadowed everything else in my life, and I felt my entire person rebelling against this fact. It is impossible for me to really express what I felt: an acute sense of precipitous disintegration, of falling headlong into absurdity and emptiness. I rebelled most of all against the image of myself that my book created. I did not want to be weak, incapable, impotent. And yet I understood that even my rebellion proved that this image was true.

In this fury of desperation I felt weightless and I moved around the room as if floating, like a leaf carried by a violent wind. I was no longer aware of my movements or of my own thoughts. The idea of running to my wife in this state of anxiety, of finding perhaps not a consolation but a straw to hang onto in the midst of this flood probably materialized in my mind before I translated it into action. But it is true that I was not aware of it before I had already opened the door of the sitting room, crossed the landing, and was standing at her door. I knocked, and realized as I did so that the door was not completely closed but ajar and I was struck, I do not know why, by the seeming artfulness of its having been left in this position. There was no response to my two knocks, and so I knocked again more loudly and, after a reasonable pause, pushed the door open and went in.

The room was dark; I turned on the ceiling lamp and in the pale light, I immediately saw her nightgown on the untouched bed, spread on the covers, arms wide. It occurred to me that she had been unable to sleep and had decided to go down to the garden, but at the same time I could not help feeling a slight irritation. She could have knocked, told me she was going: Why go alone? I glanced at the alarm clock on the nightstand and was surprised to see that almost three hours had passed from the moment I had asked my wife to kiss the title page of my book. The events that followed had occurred so quickly that I felt as if only a half hour had passed. I left her room and went downstairs.

The red and blue glass panes of the sitting-room door were illuminated; the entire house seemed awake. I went to the sitting room, certain that I would find my wife there, but it was empty. The book she had been reading for the past few days was on the table upside down and open, as if she had just paused in her reading. Next to the book there was an ashtray filled with long cigarette butts, stained with lipstick. It seemed that my wife had returned downstairs not long after she had said good night to me and had spent the evening reading and smoking. Then she must have stepped out for a walk in the garden; but it seemed that she had just done so because the air was still filled with smoke despite the open door. Perhaps I could still catch up with her. I went out onto the gravel drive.

The white light of the moon on the gravel reminded me of our walk the night before near the sharecropper's house. All of a sudden, in my state of desperate exaltation, I felt the desire to do what I had not been able to do the night before. I wanted to make love to Leda on the threshing floor, under that magnificent full moon, in the silence of the sleeping countryside, with all the passion bred of my feeling of impotence. The impulse to do this was perfectly natural, logical, and common; but this time I was content to allow myself to feel and act like a farmer who seeks comfort and recompense for the ravages of a storm in the sweetness of the conjugal embrace. After all, in the midst of the catastrophe of my ambition, my only hope was to accept my human condition, similar in every way to that of all men. After that night, I would accept that I was a good man with a certain knowledge of literature, fully and modestly conscious of his own limits, but loved by and in love with a beautiful, young wife. I would focus my unhappy passion for poetry on her. Because I was unable to write about it, I would poetically live out my amorous experience. Women love failed men who have renounced all ambition except to make them happy.

As I thought this, I began to walk down the lane, absorbed in my thoughts, head down. Then I looked up and saw Leda. Or rather I caught a glimpse of her as, far ahead, she turned the corner and disappeared. At that moment a moonbeam traversed the lane. For a moment I could distinctly see her white dress, the low neckline, and her blonde hair. Then she disappeared, and I became convinced that she was walking toward the farmhouse. It pleased me to think that she was going to the hill, where I wanted to make love to her, as if to an appointment, without knowing that the appointment was with me. I turned the corner as well and saw her again as she took a smaller side lane which, as I knew, led to the path between the fields and the garden. I was about to call out to her but held back, thinking that I would catch up to her and surprise her with my embrace.

I had reached the narrow lane when she began to walk down the path, and when I came to the path, she had already reached the hill on which the farm buildings stood. She was almost running now and her white figure in flight among the dark shadows of the trees inspired a feeling of strangeness in me. When I reached the area beneath the farmhouse, I stopped, struck by a shadowy presentiment. I could see her climbing the hill toward the threshing floor on which the round bundles of straw were piled. She grabbed onto bushes, leaning forward, slipping, and tripping, and in her intense, eager expression, dilated eyes, and the movements of her body, I could once again perceive the resemblance to a goat, climbing up a hill in search of food. When she arrived at the top of the hill, a man's figure emerged from the darkness, bent forward, took her by the arm, and lifted her up. Twisting his body in order to steady her, he turned toward me, and I recognized Antonio.

At this point I understood the situation clearly, and I felt frozen. At the same time I was filled with amazement that I had not understood the situation earlier. Not just now when I had gone into her room and found it empty, but twenty days earlier when she had asked me to fire the barber. This reflexive amazement was mixed with a dreadful malaise that left me breathless and oppressed my heart. I wanted to look away, if only out of self-respect, but instead I avidly opened my eyes even wider. After Leda stood up again, I saw the man grab her arm in an attempt to pull her toward him, and she twisted her body and resisted, pulling away. The moon illuminated her face, and I saw that it was twisted in the mute and intense grimace that I had noticed many times before. Her mouth was half-open in a sneer halfway between disgust and desire, her eyes were wide open, and her chin was thrust forward. Meanwhile, her entire body seconded the grimace with an energetic contortion, as if sketching a kind of dance.

Antonio pulled her toward him, and she resisted, pulling away. And then, I'm not sure how, she turned her back to him, he grabbed her by the elbows, and she twisted her body again, writhing with her back against him, throwing herself back into his arms while still denying him her lips. I noticed that even as she contorted her body spasmodically, she stood on the tips of her toes, and again I thought of a dance. They continued to writhe, one behind the other, for some time until they changed positions, as if dancing to a different minuet; now they were side by side. Her arm lay across his chest and he grasped her hips as she leaned toward him, head thrown back. Then they slid against each other and stood face to face. She leaned her head and chest away from him as he held her, and at the same time she lifted her dress, revealing her legs and groin. For the first time I saw that her legs were the legs of a dancer, pale, muscular, and lean, her taut feet balanced on the tips of her toes. She pulled her chest away while thrusting her groin toward his; he stood still, attempting to pull her straight and embrace her. The moon illuminated them, and now it looked as if they were really performing some kind of dance, with him standing immobile and straight as she revolved around him. It was a silent dance, without rules, but even so it followed its own furious rhythm. Finally she threw him off balance, or he stumbled on purpose, and they fell backward, disappearing together in the shadow of one of the haystacks.

CHAPTER XV

I WAS ALMOST SORRY TO see them disappear. The moon shone radiantly between the two darkened haystacks on the now empty threshing floor, where I had seen them dance one against the other, and for a moment I thought that I had not seen my wife and the barber but rather two nocturnal spirits brought forth by the moonlight. I was overwhelmed by what I had seen but attempted to be objective, and in this I was aided by my estheticism; for the first time I felt I was being put to the ultimate test. I recalled how the night before, the glimmer of the moon on the threshing floor had inspired in me the idea of frenzied lovemaking in the mild, silent night, and I understood that I had been right to think and desire this. But, at the last minute, someone else had taken my place. I had divined the beauty of that embrace, but the embrace had occurred without me.

I became suspicious that this effort at objectivity was simply an expedient of my wounded pride, and I told myself that no matter how much I reasoned and rationalized, the truth remained: I had been brutally betrayed, my wife had betrayed me with a barber, this betrayal now stood between me and my wife. At this thought, I felt a deep pain, and I realized that for the first time since I had seen Leda in Antonio's arms, I was being forced into the obligatory role of the husband of an adulterous wife. But at the same time I understood that I neither wanted to nor could remain in that role for long. I had to continue to reason and above all to understand. This was my vocation, and not even betrayal could justify my forsaking it. As I ran toward the villa, I began to doggedly reconstruct what had taken place between my wife, Antonio, and me.

Of course the man was a libertine, but it was possible that at first he had had no ill intentions; perhaps the first contact with my wife had been accidental. Similarly, it was possible that she had truly and sincerely been offended by what she had called the barber's lack of respect, even if the excessiveness of her indignation already hid the seed of an unconscious confusion and attraction. In reality, she had pleaded with me to defend her not against Antonio but against herself, but I had not understood her and had selfishly thought only of my own interest. She had not understood the selfishness of my conduct, just as she had not understood the profound motives of her own, and so she had accepted the situation, as always, out of affection and kindness. She had endured the daily presence of this man who had insulted her and to whom she did not realize she was violently attracted. Many days had gone by. Meanwhile, our passions and disagreements had been artificially suspended because of my selfish desire to finish my work, and this suspension had ultimately deepened our disagreements and matured our passions. After twenty days, my work was finished but my wife had reached, perhaps unconsciously, the extreme limit of her cloudy, shadowy desire. And thus my trip to the city had given her the opportunity to discover the true meaning of her initial reaction to the barber.

Antonio had arrived while I was out, and somehow the two of them had crossed paths, on the stairs or in the sitting room; perhaps he had approached her, or perhaps she had taken the initiative. In any case, a sudden, complete, definitive understanding had been created between them. From that moment on, Leda's conduct had exhibited the inflexibility, velocity, and weight of a stone hurtling through space toward the bottom of a ravine. Her perhaps intentional cruelty had driven her to arrange a meeting with Antonio in the same spot where just the night before I had desired to make love to her. Once Antonio had left the house, she had behaved with cold, brutal determination, laying aside the subtlety of discretion, sensitivity, or even of simple good taste, exhibiting the attitude of an enemy rather than that of a loving wife. She had made sure that I would be working that night when she went to her assignation, and she had played with me like a cat, recounting the story of her adventure with the officer, which clearly concealed her encounter earlier that day with Antonio. That night as she dressed she had taken care not to wear the elastic American girdle, so that she would be swifter, more naked, more seductive. While I ate she had made no attempt to conceal the sharp edge of her impatience, not even deigning to resort to the hypocrisy that in these situations represents a nod if not to virtue at least to good manners. Only my complete blindness could explain the fact that I had not understood that her lack of appetite was caused by another, far more overwhelming hunger. Worried that I would take her supposed indisposition too seriously and perhaps try to attend to her in her room, she had cynically attributed it to her menses. When the time came, she ran to her assignation, and the dance that I had witnessed was only the final explosion of the potent and long repressed mechanism of her desire.

I must say at this point that in Leda's behavior I could make out the illusory, ephemeral determination that erupts suddenly from the depths of our consciousness and then is reabsorbed by it, like a river in the desert. I recognized, in other words, the furious but short-lived impetus for these involuntary infractions of a recognized law. What had occurred between her and Antonio did not in any way affect her relation with me. Her intrigue with the barber, which in all probability would not survive the night, and the ties that bound her to me, now a year old, were two completely different things, on two completely different planes. I was sure that if I said nothing, Leda would continue to love me as she had before and perhaps more, and that she herself would find a way to rid herself of Antonio the very next day, if she had not done so already. But these reflections did not console me, as they should have, but rather depressed me even more. This was yet another indication of my incapacity, weakness, impotence. Not only art but my own wife offered themselves to me out of pity, affection, kindness, and tame goodwill. The fruit of this concession would never be love or poetry, but a forced and decorous composure, a tepid and chaste happiness. The real masterpiece, the dance on the threshing floor, was for another man. I was forever doomed to mediocrity.

Meanwhile, carried by my sorrow as by a wind, I had crossed the garden, entered the house, climbed the stairs, and returned to my desk. And there I was, pen in hand, sitting in front of a sheet of paper on which I had written, "Dear Leda." It was a letter of farewell to my wife. I realized I was crying.

I don't know how long I cried, only that I cried and wrote at the same time, and that as I wrote, the tears fell on the words, blurring them. I wanted to tell her that everything was finished between us and that it was better if we separated, but even as I thought and wrote these things, I experienced an intense pain and refusal with my entire body that expressed itself in an endless flood of tears. I realized that I was attached to her, that I did not care that she had betrayed me and that in the end I would not have cared if she gave herself to others for love and reserved for me a simple feeling of affection. I imagined my life without her and it occurred to me that, after having considered suicide for so many years, now I would finally go through with it. Even so, I continued to write and to cry. I finished the letter and signed it. But when I tried to reread it I realized that the tears had erased the words, and I knew that I would never have the courage to give it to her.

At that moment I clearly perceived the weakness in my character, a combination of impotence, morbidness, and selfishness, and all at once I accepted it. I realized that after that night I would be more humble and that, if I truly desired it, I could perhaps not change but at least correct myself, because during that one night I had learned more about my character than in all the preceding years of my life. This thought consoled me. I stood up from my desk, went to my room, and splashed cold water on my red, swollen eyes. Then I returned to the sitting room and gazed out of the window at the drive.

I stood there motionless for about ten minutes, thinking of nothing and allowing the silence and the serenity of the night to calm the tumult of my emotions. I was no longer thinking about Leda and was surprised to see her suddenly appear on the edge of the drive, running toward the door. She held up her long dress with both hands, and as I watched her from above, dashing across the drive illuminated by the moon, she made me think of a wild animal, like a wolf or a weasel, furtive, its fur still stained with blood, running back to its den after an incursion into a chicken coop. This impression was so strong that I could almost see her as an animal, and for a moment I sensed her innocence as a physical quality, almost like a wild musk. And despite myself I could not help but smile affectionately. Still running, she looked up toward me as I stood in the window. Our eyes met, and I thought I could see the presentiment of an unpleasant scene in her eyes. She immediately lowered them and came into the house. Slowly, I moved away from the window and sat down on the sofa.

CHAPTER XVI

A MOMENT LATER THE DOOR opened, and she entered impetuously. I recognized this aggressive stance as a defense, and I was unable to keep from smiling again. She asked, with her hand still on the door, "What are you doing? Not working?"

Without raising my head, I answered, "No."

"I went for a walk in the garden, I couldn't sleep," she said, supplying an explanation I had not requested. "What's wrong?"

She approached the desk. But clearly she did not dare come any closer. Standing next to the desk, she looked at the pages that were spread all around. With effort I said, "Tonight I've made a definitive discovery . . . which will have a profound effect on my life."

I looked at her. Still standing next to the desk, she focused her frowning eyes, which looked dilated as if by anger, on the typewriter. In a louder voice, she asked, "What discovery?"

She's preparing to respond in kind, I reflected. Her attitude reminded me of certain insects that, when in danger, rise up aggressively on their hind legs; among naturalists this is known as the "spectral attitude." I could already hear her voice crying out, "Yes, I gave myself to the barber, I like him! . . . Now you know . . . do what you like!" I sighed and added, "After rereading my story I've realized that it is worthless and that I will never be a writer."

I saw her stand still and silent, incredulously, at these words, which were so different from the ones she had expected to hear. Then she exclaimed, with some harshness still in her voice, "What are you saying?"

"I'm saying the truth," I responded calmly. "I was living on false hopes. . . . The story, which seemed like a masterpiece as I was writing it, was actually stillborn . . . and I am an unredeemable mediocrity."

She touched her forehead with her hand and slowly walked over and sat down next to me. She was clearly trying to switch to her new role, unexpected and difficult as it was, and she did so with effort. "But, Silvio, you were so sure."

"Now I am sure of the opposite," I answered, "so much so that for a moment I thought I might kill myself."

As I said this I raised my eyes to look at her. And now I understood that all this time I had spoken of my story, I had been thinking of her. I no longer cared that my story was deficient, but I could not suppress a strong wave of sadness as I observed the evidence of her tryst with Antonio, visible in her entire person. Her hair was out of place, with curls falling messily around her face, and I thought I could even see a few bits of hay here and there. The little bunch of flowers was gone; it had probably fallen on the threshing floor. Her mouth was pale and colorless, but the smudges of lipstick gave her entire face a fatigued, disconsolate air. The dress was crumpled and there was a fresh mud stain at the knee, as if she had fallen.

I realized that she was aware of her state and that she had shown herself to me like this on purpose. It would have been easy for her to go to her room first, clean herself, powder her face, remove the dress, and put on her robe. At this thought I felt another pang, as if tormented by an arrogant, merciless hostility. As I thought this, she said, "Kill yourself? You're mad . . . just because of a story that did not turn out as you had hoped?"

I translated her words in my mind: "Because of a momentary waywardness . . . because I was unable to resist a fleeting temptation," and I said to her, "For me this story was very important . . . now I am finished as a man. . . . I have the proof . . . this manuscript." And as I said this I made a brusque and almost involuntary gesture, not toward the desk where my manuscript lay, but toward her.

This time she understood me (or perhaps she had already understood and was still hoping to trick me) and she lowered her eyes in a state of confusion. She moved one of her hands, which had lain on her lap, toward her knee to hide the mud stain. Physical love exhausts the body, and certain attempts at simulation depend on physical movement. At that moment, hampered by the weariness of her senses and by the disorder of her body, she must have found it extremely difficult to take hold of herself and play the part of the affectionate wife. I feared a clumsy response and decided to tell her the truth. But then I heard her voice, unexpectedly intrepid, asking me, "Why finished? Did you not think of me?"

For a moment, I lingered on the feeling of amazement caused by these words. Her question revealed more than audacity and cleverness, admirable in themselves, perhaps, but only as an indication of unusual quickness; it revealed, or at least so it seemed to me, a touching sincerity. I asked her, "What can you do about it? You can't give me the talent that I lack."

"No," she said with her habitual, reasonable naiveté, "but I love you."

She held out her hand, seeking mine, and stared at me; her eyes seemed to become more clear and luminous as her feelings for me emboldened her and overcame her confusion. I took her hand, kissed it, and fell to my knees before her. I said softly, "And I love you, by now you should know that . . . but I'm afraid that this love may not be enough."

I held my face against the legs which a few moments before I had seen naked, improvising a dance of desire on the threshing floor, and tried to decipher the meaning of her words in my mind. I thought what I had heard was: "I made a mistake, I was overwhelmed by desire . . . but I love you, and only this matters to me . . . I repent and I won't do it again."

Everything was just as I had imagined it. But now I no longer wanted to reject this affection, no matter how inadequate. I heard her say, "When you experience these feelings of despair, you must try to think of me . . . after all, we love each other, and that is important."

Softly, I answered, "You ask me to think of you . . . do you think of me?"

"Always."

I told myself that she was not lying. She probably did always think of me, had always thought of me, even when, a moment earlier, she had let herself be taken by Antonio on the threshing floor. I could have dwelled on the ridiculous aspect of her thinking of me in such a continuous, ineffectual manner that did not stop her from betraying me and which, as is sometimes the case, had perhaps rendered the betrayal even more tempting and pleasing. But I preferred to tell myself that she really did think of me all the time, in the way one thinks of an unresolved issue that is always vivid in one's mind and is the center of one's deepest anxieties. With kindness, perhaps, but I preferred to think that outside her kindness everything in her was dark and turbid and led her to lose herself in temptations like the one that had thrust her into Antonio's arms. We were speaking different languages; I did not ascribe any importance to her kindness, which was made up of rationality and common sense, and instead attributed great importance to instinct, without which I believed that both love and art were impossible. In contrast, she ascribed importance only to this kindness, which—I thought—she believed to be the best part of herself, and rejected instinct as a defect and a fault. I reflected that one always loves what one lacks: she, who was all turbid instinct, was compelled to venerate clear thinking, while I, who was all bloodless rationality, was of course attracted by the richness of instinct. I surprised myself by murmuring, "What about art? Can art be made out of kindness?"

She caressed my head and could not have heard these words which I had murmured softly; but after a moment, she spoke as if she had heard them, in a self-possessed, spirited, affectionate tone, "Come on, get up . . . you know what we'll do? I'll go . . . I'll get undressed and climb into bed . . . then you can bring the story and read it to me . . . that way we'll see if it truly is as bad as you say."

As she said this, she stood up with a vigorous movement. I also stood, still confused, protesting that there was no point, that I knew the story was bad and that there was nothing to be done about it. But she interrupted me, covering my mouth with her hand, exclaiming, "Come, come . . . we'll see . . . now I'll go to my room and then you will join me." Before I could say anything, she was gone.

I was alone, and went to the desk and mechanically picked up the manuscript. I thought to myself that her kindness had become even more pronounced and that there was no doubt that it was sincere. Could I be sure that this kindness would triumph against the next temptation? I realized that only the future could answer that question.

I lit a cigarette and smoked without moving as I stood beside the desk. When it seemed enough time had elapsed, I walked out of the sitting room with the manuscript under my arm and knocked on her door. She immediately called out to me to come in, in a ringing, joyful voice.

She was already in bed, her chest above the covers, wearing a magnificent openwork nightgown adorned with lace. The room was dark except for one side of the bed, which was bathed in the light of the lamp on the nightstand. She was sitting, propped on the pillows, her arms lying on the covers, welcoming and ready. Her face was perfectly made up, with all her curls in place and a new bunch of fresh flowers at her left temple. She was very beautiful, and her beauty seemed to emanate from the scintillating and mysterious serenity of her face. I was struck as I looked at her by the thought that just moments before, this calm, luminous face had been deformed in the scarlet sneer of sexual desire. She smiled and said, "Come now . . . I've put on my loveliest nightgown for the occasion."

I sat on the edge of the bed, at an angle, and said, "I'll read it to you because you asked me to . . . but I've already told you that it's no good."

"Come now, I'm listening."

I picked up the first page and began to read. I read the entire story without stopping, only glancing at her once in a while as she listened, serious and attentive. As I read, my first opinion was confirmed: the story was a decorous bauble and nothing more. But this decorousness, which earlier had seemed a pointless detail, now, I'm not sure why, acquired a greater relevance than I had imagined. Still, this slightly less negative impression did not distract me from my greatest preoccupation, which was my wife. I wondered what she would say when I finished reading. I thought that she might take one of two possible paths.

She might exclaim, "Silvio, what do you mean, it's a wonderful story!" or she might admit that the story was mediocre. The first was the path of indifference and betrayal. By making me believe that the story was good, while knowing (as she surely would) that it was not, she would have clearly demonstrated that she meant to lead me by the nose, that between us there was only a rapport of falseness and compassion. The second was the path of love, her own kind of love, built out of kindness and affection. I anxiously wondered what path she would take. I decided that if she said that the story was good, I would cry out, "The story is a failure, and you are a whore!"

With this in mind I read the whole story; as I approached the end, my pace slackened, fearing what would happen. Finally I read the last sentence. "That's the end," I said, lifting my eyes to hers.

We looked at each other silently, and, like a passing cloud in a clear sky, I saw the shadow of falseness pass over her face. For a moment she considered lying to me, crying out that the story was good and revealing herself to be cold and astute by offering me the false consolation of merciful praise. But this shadow disappeared almost as soon as it had come, seemingly replaced by the love she felt for me, which was made up of truthfulness and respect. She said, in a sincerely disheartened tone, "Perhaps you're right . . . it's not the masterpiece you meant to write . . . but it's not as bad as you think now . . . it's not devoid of interest."

I responded, filled with a sense of relief, almost joy, "Didn't I tell you?"

"It's well written."

"Good writing is not enough."

"But perhaps," she said, "you didn't work on it enough . . . if you revise it, several times . . . in the end it will be the way you want it."

So it was clear that she thought that even in art, kindness and effort were more important than the gift of instinct. I said, "But I want it to be what it is; it must be the result of an inspiration, or the lack thereof. And if there is no inspiration, there is no point working or applying oneself."

She exclaimed excitedly, "That's where you're wrong. You don't ascribe enough importance to work and application . . . they are very important. Things are accomplished mostly through work and application and not at random, as if by a miracle."

We argued for a while longer, both of us steadfastly convinced of our completely opposite points of view. Finally, I folded the manuscript in four and put it in my pocket saying, "Let's not talk about it anymore."

There was a moment of silence. Then I said, gently, "Are you disappointed that you are married to a failed writer?"

She answered quickly, "I have never thought of you as a writer."

"And what did you think of me then?"

Smiling, she said, "Oh, I don't know . . . what can I say? I know you too well now . . . I know how you are . . . you are always the same to me . . . whether you write or not."

"But if you had to, how would you judge me?"

She hesitated, then said sincerely, "One can't judge when one loves someone."

So we always returned to the same point. The obstinacy of her protestations of love moved me. I took her hand and said, "You're right . . . I also love you, and because of this I cannot judge you, though I know you well."

With a knowing spark in her eyes, she exclaimed, "You see? When one loves a person, one loves everything about that person . . . even the defects."

I would have liked to say to her, with all sincerity, "I love you the way you are now, sitting on the bed, calm, serene, with your lovely nightgown, your curls, your bunch of flowers, and your luminous, limpid eyes, and I love you the way you were moments ago when you danced with desire and gnashed your teeth and pulled up your dress as Antonio embraced you . . . and I will always love you." But I said nothing because I realized that she had understood that I knew everything and that everything was now resolved between us. Instead, I said, "One day, perhaps, I'll rewrite the story . . . the last word hasn't been said . . . when I feel ready to express certain things."

She said vividly, "I'm also convinced you should rewrite it . . . someday."

I wished her good night, kissed her, and went off to sleep. I slept soundly, a deep, bitter sleep, like a child after being punished by his parents for some mischievousness or willfulness, after having cried and screamed for a long time, and after finally being forgiven. The following morning, I awoke late, shaved myself, and, after breakfast, I suggested to my wife that we go for a stroll before lunch. She agreed, and we went out together.

Just above the sharecropper's farmhouse, at the top of the hill, stood the ruins of a small church. We climbed up a mule track to the ruin and sat on the low wall that marked the churchyard, gazing out at the view. The church was very old, as one could judge from the Romanesque capitals on the columns that supported the external portico. Other than this portico, all that remained of the church were sections of the walls, the ruined apse, and an almost unrecognizable stump which had once been the bell tower. The churchyard, paved with ancient gray stones, was overtaken with weeds, and beneath the small portico, through the cracks between the boards of the roughly hewn door, one could glimpse vigorous, leafy weeds in the sunlight, growing in clumps in the apse. I inspected the church and noticed that there was a face or mask sculpted in the stone of one of the capitals. The elements had corroded and smoothed the rough sculpture, rendering it almost formless, but one could still distinguish the frowning expression of a demon of the kind created by sculptors of bas-reliefs in order to admonish the faithful. In this ancient, semi-erased grimace, I was struck by a distant similarity with the sneer I had seen on my wife's face the previous night. Yes, it was the same grimace, and that stonecutter from long ago had surely meant to allude to the same kind of temptation by stressing the plaintive sensuality of the thick lips and the fiery expression of the eyes. I looked away from the capital, toward Leda. She was contemplating the landscape and seemed lost in thought. Then she turned toward me and said, "Listen, last night I thought about your story . . . I think I understand now why it is unconvincing."

"Why?"

"You meant to write about us, isn't that right?"

"Yes, in a way."

"Well, you started from a false premise . . . one can feel that when you wrote the story you did not know me well enough, or yourself . . . perhaps it was too soon to write about us and our relationship, it was too early. . . . Especially me, you represented me differently from how I really am . . . I was too idealized."

"So?"

"Well, that's it . . . I think that after some time, when we know each other better, you should try again, just as you said last night . . . I'm sure you'll write something good."

I said nothing and simply caressed her hand. Meanwhile, over her shoulder I looked at the capital and the demon and thought that in order to rewrite the story I would have to know the devil as well as the unknown stonecutter, but also its opposite. "It will take a long time," I said softly, finishing my thought aloud.

Printed in the United States
By Bookmasters